CONFESSIONS OF A POACHIN PARSON...

Tall Tales
and Short Stories
From a Circuit Riding Preacher

by

Dun Gordy

Illustrations
by
Bruce Day
Pill Pittenger
Katrina Smith

Published by

Circuit Rider Ministries

in cooperation with

TRAFFORD

Canada • UK • Ireland • USA • Spain

Note for Librarians: a cataloguing record for this book that
includes Dewey Decimal Classification and US Library
of Congress numbers is available from the Library and
Archives of Canada. The complete cataloguing record can
be obtained from their online database at:
www.collectionscanada.ca/amicus/index-e.html
ISBN 1-4120-3080-3

TRAFFORD

Offices in Canada, USA, Ireland, UK and Spain
This book was published on-demand in cooperation
with Trafford Publishing. On-demand publishing is a
unique process and service of making a book available for
retail sale to the public taking advantage of on-demand
manufacturing and Internet marketing. On-demand
publishing includes promotions, retail sales, manufacturing,
order fulfilment, accounting and collecting
royalties on behalf of the author.
Book sales in Europe:
Trafford Publishing (UK) Ltd., Enterprise House,
Wistaston Road Business Centre, Wistaston Road,
Crewe CW2 7RP UNITED KINGDOM
phone 01270 251 396 (local rate 0845 230 9601)
facsimile 01270 254 983; info.uk@trafford.com
Book sales for North America and international:
Trafford Publishing, 6E–2333 Government St.,
Victoria, BC V8T 4P4 CANADA
phone 250 383 6864 (toll-free 1 888 232 4444)
fax 250 383 6804; email to bookstore@trafford.com
or contact the author at dungordy@earthlink.net or
order online at www.trafford.com/robots/04-0907.html

10 9 8 7 6 5

This was first published in the GOOD NEWS BROADCASTER, May, 1985. But it is more true and appropriate today than ever before! And it is for that reason that I have chosen to insert it here as the

Dedication

TO MY BEST FRIEND

I sometimes think that I really have it hard in the ministry as a travelling mission representative. I travel many, many miles and I am away from home much of the time.

But as I breeze along in air-conditioned comfort I listen to great sermons or good music on my stereo, uninterrupted by doorbells, telephones or demanding children.

I drive through or fly over some of the most beautiful scenery in God's creation and am fed like the rich man in Luke who fared sumptuously every day.

I am graciously received by God's people like a visiting ambassador and praised as the greatest, the funniest, the most this-or-that by congregations who would think Balaam's donkey to be dynamic after having listened to the same pastor for years.

Always seated at the head table at banquets, I am usually the first through the line at potluck suppers.

Because I am the visiting preacher I am given the best bed in the house even if my host has to sleep on the rollaway in the children's room (which I don't even find out until the next day).

When I leave, I am presented with a generous offering as a love gift from people who really do love me.

But I suppose that the worst part is when people make a martyr of me because I have to be away from my family so much, have to sleep in so many different beds and drive so many miles.

All this is true just because I have come in Someone's place to give a message. There I stand: honored, praised, pampered and paid.

I shamefully admit that sometimes it takes its toll. But just as quickly as I am tempted by the flesh to give in to Satan's clever device, I am delivered from that snare by God's mercy. And more often than not it is by His gentle reminder that the greatest reason for my effectiveness is that part of me that the congregation never sees. I am useable because of YOU. Though I would have the tongue of men and angels, even if I were dynamic and eloquent, and if I were as praiseworthy as some think, without you I would be nothing.

Before He gave me the gift of preaching and before He developed in me the abilities and talents to do His work, He gave me the most essential of all. He gave me His own child whom He had made after the pattern of Proverbs 31:10-31.

Many wives have done virtuously, but my dear wife sure excels them all. You are a rare jewel indeed who serves God in this noblest of all ministries the wife of an itinerant preacher. You are not praised except by your husband.

When I speak before a congregation of hundreds, you are a thousand miles away with a dirty diaper in one hand and a squirming child in the other. You are unrecognized except as the smiling face on the prayer card. As I am in the midst of a crowd of admirers pointing out which child is the oldest and which one I was talking about in my sermon, you may be in the midst of brushing your teeth while both the telephone and the doorbell are ringing. On the phone you are recognized as being the mother of that brat who just punched Johnny in the mouth. At the door our daughter wants to show you the big frog she just caught.

While I am honored as having so much Bible knowledge about the third toe on the left foot of Daniel's beast, you are home praying for wisdom to handle such insignificant trivia as how to get the old car running in time to get to prayer meeting.

As I am graciously receiving the generous check from the deacon you are home digging thru all your old purses to find a quarter for the collection they are taking to buy our son's coach a birthday present.

To the congregations who praise and honor me you are known only as my wife, the mother of our children. You are just a picture on a prayer card. My good works are seen and praised before men. I am recognized and rewarded. Your service is most often in secret and goes unnoticed by the world. I want you to know that it is not totally unnoticed. I notice. It is I who am the recipient of your labor of love. It is I who could never begin to minister effectively if it were not for you.

And our loving Heavenly father notices. Not only notices but also He promises that thy Father which seeth in secret Himself shall reward thee openly.

I want to thank you for being the wife God wants you to be. Because of your faithfulness the Savior is able to use us in His great work. I love you, Dear. I thank God for the privilege of being your fellow servant as well as your loving husband.

Table of Contents

PART I
THE POLE CREEK RIDGE GANG

PART II
EVERYONE IN FLORIDA IS FROM SOMEWHERE ELSE

PART III
LEST WE FORGET THOSE MEMORABLE MICE!

PART I

THE POLE CREEK RIDGE GANG

THE POLE CREEK RIDGE GANG

Now, you know preachers don't tell lies. At least they aren't supposed to. And for the most part they don't. I'm sure you personally know an exception to the rule and if you don't, you won't have to look very far for someone who can give you all the evidence, real or made up, to amply supply you. So I want to start off right up front and tell you that a preacher wrote this passage of absolutely essential nonsense. And I want to personally guarantee you that every word you read will be the purely fabricated and well-garnished *truth* based on solid and verifiable *fiction*. I have, by necessity, taken the liberty to change the names of some of the folk just to protect their guilt.

You see, I am also a sometime fisherman and an every-chance-I-get hunter. In fact, I hold a charter membership in one of the most notorious and exclusive sporting clubs in all of North America. And it is because of my frequent association with fellow members that I sometimes have difficulty handling the truth without taking some awful liberties with it. You would too, if you hung around with the likes of this crew.

Our senior member, senior because of age, is Parnelli Pettigrew whom every one calls Nellie. As you can imagine, the other kids had tormented him in school calling him Petticoat. And because of that, even a girl-sounding name like Nellie wasn't so aggravating to him as it might have been to some other fellow. Since retirement from the mill, he's had more cabin time than the rest of us. Maybe sometime I'll tell you why his wife Josie will never join us. Actually, she doesn't trust any one of us separated nor together - especially together. And that includes her own husband! Truth is, I think she'd rather be seen with the worst chicken thief in town than to be known as one of our associates. Of course, she won't mind going to church with us or even around in well-lighted areas of town and in large crowds like the annual Christmas parade. But only then if it is obvious we are not functioning in our association as club members.

Then there's Archibald Jackson Jones. He's a deacon in the Baptist church and… well, I really don't want to tell you too much about what he does for a living. If I gave enough identifying information it would destroy any unwarranted confidence you may have in our elected government officials.

Everybody affectionately calls his wife Roberta, Peg Leg. One leg was in a cast for the first couple of years in school due to an accident as a child. I really don't even know exactly how it all happened. It had something to do with an ornery old sow and a billy goat she and her brother were going to enter in a Sunday School contest of some sort. The only time I asked her father about it, he told me that much before he broke up in such uncontrollable crying laughter we thought we were going to have to get him to the hospital for oxygen and a sedative.

My wife Harriet is of course one of the charter members. She is as southern as grits and as sweet as Alabama cane syrup. She is about as naive as a puppy and holds the club record for the biggest legally caught bass. You need take note of the fact that I said *legally caught* as opposed to the actual largest one taken by another member who shall remain anonymous until the statute of limitations has expired.

Some folks believe that Doc found his license to practice in a Cracker Jacks box. And others will swear that he could deliver live healthy twin calves from a cow that had been lying dead in the sun for 3 days. I won't comment on that but I warn you not to try to keep up with that short-legged old man when he's hunting chukkas nor following a bull elk straight up a mountain. Docs wife Gertrude is deadly with a shotgun and has a shelf full of trophies to prove it. What makes her most loved, at least in the club is her stew! She usually sends a pot along with us to elk camp and there's no better consolation to a bloodless day of hunting than to end it with a steaming bowl full.

We have had other members come and go and a few associate members you may meet from time to time but this is the basic core. It may seem like a rather small group, but remember I told you it was one of the most exclusive. We'd like to think that it is because we are very selective about the character and the reputation of those with whom we associate. I am afraid however, that the non-member citizens of this region are much more careful and cautious about who they affiliate with. It could possibly be the inflated rate of annual dues. But actually the real truth is probably that the sheriff has just put the word out on us!

At any rate, they are just about the best bunch of folks you ever sat around a campfire with. Especially, if it was one of those fires where Peg Leg had just dished up a batch of her famous Reuben sandwiches. I tell you they'd make anybody's lips go flippity-flop. She starts out with her own whole wheat bread that she baked back home the week before buck season starts. Then she takes a jar of sour kraut that she and grandma made in an ole crock in the basement last winter. I always wondered how they knew when it was ready to transfer to the fruit jars for sealing and storing until I went down there one time. After she took the lid off I couldn't blow my nose for 3 days. Of course, I didn't have to, but the smell was in my clothes for two washings.

But back to the makings of her Reubens... She gets Gloria over at the deli to slice up some corned beef real thin. Then the same with some Swiss cheese. In my opinion, the only tolerable way to eat that stinking stuff is in one of these sandwiches which somehow makes it taste all together different. Well, she butters that bread on both sides, adds her secret ingredient which I think is store-bought thousand island dressing (but don't tell her I said so), piles on a liberal amount of meat and just the right amount of cheese, sauce and kraut and your mouth starts watering already.

You should let the cook fire die down to glowing coals before you prop the old black iron grill on the rocks - just the right height over it to cook 'em slow. The only problem is that by the time she has them ready to cook, they have slung such a craving on everybody that there ain't no way you could hold off just to wait on a perfectly good fire to burn down. So we usually end up rushing the process and burning the crust a little too black. But if you think that diminishes the absolutely delicious taste of this exquisite cuisine, you're just dumb. I honestly believe I would pay the exorbitant annual dues and continue to serve on the committee for the preservation of the pop-bottle deposit just for attendance at the annual Reuben sandwich eat out. At the first bite you almost weep with sheer pleasure and delight. If you put just a dab of one on your elbow, you'd break your arm trying to lick it off!

I have eaten fish 'n chips in London, bagels in Jerusalem, lasagna in Rome, squab in Athens, caviar in Manila and steaks in Dallas. But if I had my choice I'd even walk all the way to the top of Greenhorn Mountain for the taste of those Reubens in the company of the best folks on earth—my fellow club members.

I have had a private audience with the archbishop whose political and religious influence helped overthrow the king of Greece back in the '60s. Two state governors have known and called me by my first name and I have met two United States presidents. I have had breakfast with Hollywood movie stars, lunch with major league baseball and football players and have hob-knobbed with some of the best known preachers in the country. But the company I prefer most on this earth is this bunch of deer slaying, elk hunting, trout catching, Christmas tree thieves who can always be found on or near Pole Creek ridge the first week of October.

If I never see another sunrise, the remembrance of one particular gold and purple day we saw break over a frosty Mt. Ireland will be enough to hush me with a memory of awe and majesty.

Should some malady rob from me the sense of smell, there will linger in my mind the semi-sweet scent of buck brush in Sawmill Gulch; burned gun powder from the barrel of a smoking rifle; coffee brewing in the pre-dawn chill of hunting camp; Reuben sandwiches cooking over an open fire and the delicious smell of fresh cut evergreen boughs for Christmas decorations.

If I am never excited again, the unmistakable double click of cold steel locking a shell in the chamber; the stomp and snort of a deer just out of sight in a thicket; the crashing and pounding of an elk through a Lodge pole patch; a trophy buck with frost on his antlers staring at me -these will creep into my day-dreaming mind and bring chills to my spine even on the warmest summer night.

I can be creeping down a crowded freeway in rush-hour traffic or speeding along some lonely desert road, sitting in a pulpit waiting for my turn to preach or eating a tasteless meal in some swanky restaurant 1,000 miles from home and find myself barely - if at all - able to suppress laughter. Those around me may wonder about my sanity. In fact, they probably would have me committed if I told them "Oh, I was just remembering a jelly-bean bath in a Blazer!" or "What do you call a flat file?" Or if I said I was laughing at the manner of death of a certain Parson Brown, most folks would think me cruel. A song about a city dump hasn't made the charts but it sure brings hilarious memories of a buck in the street light and Nellie hollering "Don't shoot!" Punctuated by the roar of a rifle.

I have travelled over a lot of the real estate of our wonderful globe. I have seen the beauty of Galilee's sea and Australia's great coral reefs; from Hawaii's silver sand to Canada's magnificent Rockies; from the mighty Amazon to Niagara Falls and from the bottom of the Grand Canyon to the top of the Sears' tower. But the most beautiful sights in this world are seen from the top of Pole Creek ridge, Marble Creek pass, the knob on Greenhorn Mountain and an elk stand on ... well, I won't mention the exact location of that one.

Indian summer falls in the October deer season around these parts bringing scenery no artist with exceptional skill, sanctified paintbrush and glorified imagination could begin to do justice to. Even one of those expensive cameras with that new-fangled digital technology could only catch bits and pieces of the Creator's handiwork. Yet the thing that makes it all so wonderfully enjoyable is having someone to share it with. And God has been especially good to me by allowing me to enjoy it in the company of my dearly beloved fellow members of the POLE CREEK RIDGE ROD, RIFLE AND REUBEN SANDWICH SOCIETY.

SCATTER MY ASHES ON POLE CREEK RIDGE

The old fellow had a tendency of dozing off in church and no amount of teasing from the congregation, fussing from his wife or encouragement from the pastor could cure him of this habit. He always had a good-natured response. He assured the pastor that it was a real compliment when he slept thru the Reverends message. "I want you to know that I trust you, Parson. Don't need to stay awake to check you." With a twinkle in his eye, he proudly declared that it took a man with a clean conscience to sleep in a hell-fire, damnation sermon.

Well, one day the pastor decided he'd cure him once and for all. When he was sure the deacon was well off into that somnambulistic state of glorious oblivion he challenged the congregation to stand up if you want to go to heaven."

When the congregation realized that it was a serious invitation, they began to rise to their feet. Everyone was standing except the sleeping deacon.

This time the preacher shouted a bit louder "If you want to go to heaven, stand up!" By now the congregation realized what was happening. And in the silence that followed, the sleeping saint lifted his head.

Looking directly at him the preacher asked one more time, "Brother, I said anyone who was planning to go to heaven, stand up. Don't you want to go to heaven?"

"I heard you the first time, Preacher. I just though you were getting up a load to go tonight!"

Like most Christians, I would love to be living here on this earth when our Lord returns. Nothing against those who make their living with a business that is constantly going in the hole, but I would like to cheat the funeral folks out of mine. Yet, if I do have to leave this world like every one of my ancestors, I do not want to be buried.

16

I have already instructed my family to take out anything that still works, give it to anyone who can use it and burn the rest.

And Larry has promised that he will scatter my ashes on Pole Creek Ridge near my favorite deer stand!

THOSE NEWFANGLED SHOTGUNS

I never did know the real reason why our Parnelli Pettigrew couldn't get his wife Josie to participate in any of the activities of the Pole Creek Ridge Rod, Rifle and Reuben Sandwich Society. Josie was one of the sweetest ladies you ever met and just lots of fun to be around. But we could never get her to be involved with us if there was any suspicion that it was an official or even unofficial gathering of our most exclusive society.

Josie didn't mind going to church with us. In these most recent years she's even been known to sit with us at a ball game. At least she will sit with some of us folks if there aren't too many of us together in one area. She is serious about not being known to have any association what'soever with what she calls "That gang of good-for-nothing goons."

We were sitting around the cabin one night during elk season, having finished off almost the whole pot full of Peg Leg's world-class chili and most of the potato salad that Josie had sent. We had put on a second pot of coffee and were working our way through a plate of those peanut butter and chocolate bars that my Harriet makes so good. She sent them along erroneously thinking that they would last us the entire elk season.

Doc had been reading us excerpts from McMannus' latest book. Arch had laughed so hard he nearly lost his breath. Doc allowed as how he had better quit reading before it cost us a good elk hunting trip. We sure didn't want to be interrupted by having to take one of our members back to town for emergency medical treatment over something as silly as uncontrolled giggles.

We finally admitted among ourselves how much we missed having the women along here in elk camp. The highlight of our year is when we all get together for deer season. That's when the subject came up of Josie and her failure to enjoy the finer associations of life.

It seems her aversion to our company dates back to the early days of their marriage. In fact she and Nellie had only been married a month or so when he was first introduced to the original membership in the club. Most all of those charter members have gone on to the happy trout stream beyond the rainbow. Their legacy lingers however, and their memory always brings a sheepish grin to Nellie's face and the closest you'll ever come to a cuss word expression on the face of his sweet Christian wife.

Josie was working as a nurse at the hospital and Nellie got on at the mill. Old man Magnus was an engineer with the railroad when he wasn't bass fishing. He and Nellie were planning a bird-hunting trip when he found out that Nellie didn't even have a gun.

Now Nellie grew up poor. The family barely eked out a living on ground so sorry that you couldn't raise a flag on a pole out there. In fact, his old grandpa made them promise to put baking soda in his casket to assure his rising on the resurrection day! The only gun that Nellie had ever shot was a single barrel 12-guage that his grandpa had bought through a mail order catalog early in the century. Magnus had a hard time convincing him that they had actually built a gun that would shoot five times out of the same barrel without reloading. Wanting' to help out the young groom and new member of the club Magnus offered to let Nellie use his old 12-guage pump. Since Magnus didn't get off from the switch engine until later in the morning, Nellie was to go by the house, get the guns and ammo and meet him at the depot. They would go hunting directly from there.

The first problem began to develop when Nellie realized that he did not know how to unload this new fangled weapon. Magnus always kept it loaded with double-0 buckshot, just in case some prowler with suicidal tendencies came poking around the place. Nellie was too proud to admit it to Magnus' wife he had never used one of these newfangled guns so he decided to take it on down to the hardware store and have somebody down there help him out.

When Nellie got to the store he found that every clerk on duty that morning was already busy. He laid that gun on the counter and proceeded to browse through an old copy of *Field and Stream*. Swede

Jensen had been trying to help himself and had searched in vain for the right nut to go on a bolt he had. When he gave up in disgust he noticed Nellie standing by the counter and walked over to greet him. Swede was a charter member of the club as well and was anxious to help Nellie with his dilemma.

"Vots the trubble vith de gun?" he asked.

"No trouble with the gun," Nellie said, "it's with me. I just don't know how to unload this thing."

"Vell dats no problem. I can show you how" Swede assured him. "You yust push dis little button by de trigger and pump it back like dis He shucked the action back and forth in one smooth motion and pumped the 12 gauge shell right out on to the counter.

"That looks simple enough" Nellie said. Here, let me try.

With that he took the gun from Swede and proceeded to imitate his actions. With a couple of awkward jerks and pulls, he finally managed to flip the shell out onto the counter. The next shell slipped into place ready to be pumped into the chamber. Nellie shoved forward with his left hand to close the action.

KAAA-BBAAAA—WRROOOOOOMM!

The roar of a short-barrel twelve gauge in the confines of that hardware store was enough to deafen everyone in the place. The impact kicked Nellie like a mule, knocking him into Swede and they both pitched backwards upsetting the entire stock of nuts, bolts, screws and washers. In his desperate attempt to get away before Nellie could reload, Swede upset the pyramid of one-gallon paint cans. As the display tumbled in every direction, one of the paint cans caught Nellie across the forehead and cut just enough gash to bring a trickle of blood down his face. Another one bloodied his nose. One of the paint cans busted open and spilled crimson all over the front of Nellie's shirt and the back of Swede's pants.

When he did manage to scramble to his feet, Swede went screaming out the front door hollering in perfect, unaccented agony, "Don't shoot!! Don't shoot!!"

Mr. Johnson had not even recovered from the shock of the explosion when he saw Swede go out the front door, heard him screaming and saw the bloody seat of his britches. He grabbed the telephone and dived behind the counter calling for the sheriff. In hushed and hurried tones he reported that there was a shooting in progress. An ambulance and all the deputies they could spare were needed immediately!

Nellie managed to scramble to his feet desperately trying to see through the thick cloud of gun smoke that filled the store. There was a jagged, splintered hole in the wall behind the counter where the load of buckshot had torn through. There was a sick panic in the pit of his stomach as he envisioned the death and disaster he was surely going to find in the Blue Jay barbershop next door. He charged for the front door.

The usual calmness of the local barbershop was shattered by the deafening blast. Fortunately Mr. Jones had just stepped over to the sink to get a fresh towel when the gun went off. Just as he turned around, the cabinet behind the barber's chair exploded. The entire load of buckshot went through a brand new two-pound can of talcum powder, spraying it all over him, his customer and everything in the shop. All nine pellets of that twelve gauge double-ought buckshot went right into the dead center of the back of the barber's chair, ripping off all the beautiful leather upholstery. When it crashed into the steel plate of the chair itself, there was an awful roar, and the Baptist preacher was knocked sprawling out of the chair and across the room. Both he and Barber Jones were completely blinded by the cloud of white talcum powder that filled the room and covered them. They managed to stagger to the front door and stumbled out just as Nellie came barreling around the corner with the smoking shotgun still in his hand.

Dreading the absolute worst, Nellie was still not prepared for the sight that he met face to face. The shock of meeting the ghost of the Baptist preacher and the Presbyterian elder, enveloped in the same white cloud was more than he could handle. He fainted in mid stride and his limp body rolled head over heels like a shot-dead rabbit, coming to rest against his old pickup truck.

In the same mid-stride, the preacher and the elder saw Nellie, the panic, fear and blood on his face, the gun in his hand and they naturally concluded he'd gone bezerk and was looking for victims. To assure that they would not be next they simultaneously decided to be somewhere else as quickly as possible. The only problem was that the flowing barber's cloth the preacher still wore, hung on the doorknob and held him fast. Persuaded that the death angel was just holding him for Nellie to get a better shot, he dropped to his knees and began to pray in a loud and frantic voice as earnestly and as theologically correct as possible.

When he heard Nellie rolling past him and crash into the side of the pick up he opened his eyes. The sight of his young church member sprawled unconscious and bleeding just added more urgency to his heavenly petition. He concluded that God must have killed Nellie in quick answer to his prayer for self-preservation. So he began to repent of the selfishness and beg the Lord's forgiveness for thinking more of his own life that others.

Meanwhile, in his panicked flight to avoid execution, the barber was in a footrace for life. He got to the cafe the same time the police chief was emerging from his regular morning coffee break. Having heard the initial shotgun blast, the chief was drawing his gun as he came out the door. The barber ploughed into him, sending him sailing backwards and his gun went skidding across the sidewalk. Being hit so suddenly and so hard must have stunned him momentarily. Quickly recovering but still dazed he pointed his index finger, thumb upraised, at the barber and yelled, "Don't move or I'll shoot!"

Josie was in the middle of her shift at the hospital when the call came for the ambulance. She rushed out to the back door and dived into the ambulance with the medical kit she was assigned to bring. The driver hit the siren and his flashing lights and they sprayed gravel all over the emergency room entrance as they roared off to the rescue of citizens in distress.

The scent of gun smoke had faded and the last of the cloud of talcum powder dust was settling as the ambulance skidded to a stop. The scene was still rather confusing. The preacher still kneeling in the doorway of the barbershop was praying loudly and earnestly. Only Frank Johnson's head showed protruding from his crouched position in the hardware store. In front of the cafe, the chief of police was struggling out from under his patrol car where he had crawled in search of his gun. Inside, everyone had taken shelter under tables, behind counters and the six missing men were later rescued from the ladies restroom. Nellie was still sound asleep against the pick up.

The ambulance skidded to a stop someone yelled from across the street "Don't get out. The crazy fool might shoot you, too.

Well, at least Josie and the driver knew what the call was about now. Somebody had been shot. They didn't know who, nor how many nor how badly anyone was hurt. When the chief finally managed to free himself from the tie-rod end, which had held him under his car, he quickly took charge. He yelled instructions for the medical team to "Come see if you can help this gun-shot victim by the pick up!" He rushed to the aid of the praying preacher.

Only when she turned her attention from the clumsy stretcher to the victim they had come to help did Josie recognize her beloved groom, Nellie. Laying nearly upside down against the truck, blood all over his face and crimson paint on the front of his shirt, her nurses training told her in that split second that she was a widow. The split second just before she fainted.

It took twenty minutes to revive Josie.

It took them two days to find Swede Jensen.

The congregation said the next Lord's Day sermon was the best the preacher had ever delivered. Mr. Jones increased his giving to the Presbyterian church. The police chief took his two-week vacation early and left town the next morning.

It took Nellie and Josie a year to pay for the new barber's chair that had to be shipped from Chicago. It didn't take ten minutes to get the cafe cleaned up and ready for the lunch crowd. But for over 40 years Nellie has not been able to make sufficient atonement to his bride for his part in "the unloading".

Oh, yes. Mr. Johnson had a plaque engraved and mounted it over the repaired hole in his hardware store wall to commemorate the event:

"NO LOADING OR UNLOADING OF GUNS
DURING BARBER SHOP HOURS"

BUCK HUNTING
IN A BLACK HEARSE

Mr. Meriwether D. Harrington, Jr. was one of those rare men who looked so much like the stereotype of his profession that you'd think he was typecast for the role by a Hollywood studio. The general consensus of opinion was that this was due to the fact that he was raised in the funeral business. His father had been the founder, owner, embalmer, funeral director and everything else of the finest and most prosperous funeral home in Eastern Oregon. It was believed that Meriwether junior was actually born on the embalming table in the back room. It was a fact that he had lived, until the day of his marriage, in the apartment upstairs over the funeral home. Said marriage took place in the temporarily redecorated parlor normally used for funerals.

Nobody ever found out what the D. in his name stood for but every kid in town was sure it was "Death". As I said, he looked the part. The mid-wife attending his home birth swore that he came into this world weeping before the Doctor ever laid a hand on him. The unconfirmed rumor is that his mother actually used black diapers. But his father did have his first little black suit made for him when other boys were in knee pants.

He inherited a good financial security. In fact, his was the only company that continued to show a good profit in a business that was constantly going in the hole. Come to think of it, I never saw a funeral home that did not have all the outward signs of affluence - Cadillac hearses, chandeliers, manicured lawns and satin sheets in the coffin!

Although he had to attend school to earn his state licensee, Meriwether already knew more about the actual working of a successful funeral home that his professors. Still the easiest part of the entire course for him was the final two weeks. It was during this time that students were taught the very difficult technique of looking sad during a very expensive funeral! Because of his natural-born appearance, he breezed thru those sessions.

Now ole' Meriwether was a man who was known to be as tight with his money as he was stingy with his words. He just never talked unless it was absolutely necessary - and he was the one to determine when it was necessary.

In order to keep the expenses to the bare minimum, Meriwether and his wife did all the work in the funeral business until the children came. As soon as the young ones were big enough to help they were immediately put to work. Only on the most rare occasions did they ever hire additional help and then for the lowest wages they could get by with.

Which explains why Charlie Outhouser was working for him on that fateful night. Charlie was the oldest son of old lady Outhouser and the sometimes here, sometimes gone prospector named Gustav. They had a yard full of younguns and none of them were the brightest in the world. Charlie still lived at home with his mother and her passel of kids. He picked up odd jobs here and there from time to time. He could always depend on Mr. Harrington to send for him when someone died. He was a first class gravedigger. But no one in town would trust him with equipment more mechanical than a shovel. They might let him push a lawn mower or a wheelbarrow, provided it was an old wheelbarrow.

That is, no one but Harrington. And it is the consensus of public opinion that was because he didn't have to pay Charlie but 35 cents an hour when the minimum wage was a whole dollar.

I hate to talk about anyone, especially as regards to an area they can't do much about. But Charlie was just plain broke out with the DUMB. In fact, most folks felt that he had a double dose of it. And that was a well-known fact. To be truthful, it was a matter of public record. Military record.

For some unknown reason Charlie had volunteered for military duty. And even more astonishing is the fact that the Army took him. They sent him to some place down in Georgia for basic training that lasted less time than it takes to review his entire military career. Charlie was back on the streets of our hometown before his hair had time to grow out from the military buzz.

Nobody really knows what all Charlie must have taught the Army but the reason for his final separation and bus ticket home, Charlie told on himself. Not that he understood. He simply obeyed orders; he did exactly as he was told. But his lieutenant exploded in a fit of rage and kicked him out of the Army, Charlie declares. And to this day he cannot understand why they treated him so badly. And especially when he was the only man in the outfit who knew what the sergeant meant and did what he was told, he says.

They gave us those big old Springfield Oh-three guns to tote. They was heaaavvvy! And they wouldn't even shoot, no how. A fact that probably saved more than one life if there were many recruits like our fellow citizen Outhouser. They had an old leather strap on em but they wouldn't let us tote them by it he explained. Now the lieutenant, his gun warnt near as big a ours. It was a little bitty ole carbine and he could tote hisn by that strap hanging over his shoulder. It wasn't fair but he was the boss man in that army.

One day they made us march about ninety miles in the morning and in the afternoon we was supposed to march all the way back to camp. We took a break for a few minutes and then we got ready to march back. Well, that ole L. T. (that's what we called him when he couldn't hear us) he must a been about as tired of toting them worthless old guns as the rest of us was. In fact, he got so plumb disgusted that he up and hollered for us to SLING ARMS. Arms is what they called guns in the Army, he explained as if it were as much news to you as it was to Charlie when he enlisted.

Well, I done what he told us to do. I grabbed that Springfield by the end of the barrel and I slung that Oh-three as far as I could sling it! That thing whooshed like a helicopter when it sailed over the L. T.s head. I missed him a country mile but he squalled like he was busted. Acted like he ain't never seen nobody sling a gun before, and hed just told me to do it.

And every time he told the story Charlie had the same amazed questioning look as if he were still trying to understand why the L. T. got so mad and why the Army had sent him home. Not only did his obedient behavior get him a separation from the military, it also gave him a permanent nickname: Slingshot.

The funeral director had to go to Pendleton to bring back the remains of one of our fellow citizens whose family wanted him sent home for burial. Harrington had hired Slingshot for the amazing pay of 75 cents an hour since he would actually be driving the hearse home with the owner sitting right beside him to watch his every move.

Archibald Jackson Jones, the president, chief guide, head tracker and tail gunner of the Pole Creek Ridge Gang had started college right out of high school. They gave him a scholarship at the college over in Pendleton and he worked hard to prove that he deserved it. He was majoring in forestry and had a natural ability as well as a great love for anything that grew beyond the end of the pavement and city lights.

Arch thoroughly enjoyed his time in school. Unlike a lot of the other fellows there, he had gone to learn all he could about the profession he had always wanted to spend his life in. Otherwise there would have been no way he would have been content to be so far from North Powder. He was a good student.

But above and beyond and besides all else, Arch was, and is to this day, an incurable buck hunter. So when the season finally rolled around that year, he was diligent to get all his assignments in and even worked a week ahead in order not to miss opening day on a wind-swept ridge in Baker County.

The fact that his ole' pick-up truck wouldn't start that Friday afternoon was just the foreshadowing of a memorable weekend. In spite of all he could do to coax the ancient 'Chevy into life, it simply sat there and growled at him as he romped the starter. After checking everything he knew to look at, he finally decided to abandon the thing and get home the best way he could.

By now, all the other fellows from Baker County had been long gone. The train had just left and the next Greyhound wasn't due until Saturday morning that would get him to North Powder too late to catch a ride to the woods with his Dad. The only option was to head out to the highway and stick out his thumb. Surely someone would give a clean-cut college kid a ride home.

So, zipping up his jacket against the cold and pulling the flaps of his cap down over his ears, he set our across town at a fast walk. The snow, which had been falling all day, made walking difficult but not impossible. Especially to a fellow who was going hunting. The temperature began to drop even faster than the sun had disappeared. When Arch finally made his way thru town it was long past suppertime. He cut across the parking lot and ducked into the inviting warmth of the truck stop for a burger and steaming cup of coffee. He really wanted hot chocolate but they would refill an empty coffee mug free. And he needed plenty of caffeine to brace himself for the long night ahead.

As he stomped the snow off his boots inside the front door, he was nearly knocked down by old man Meriwether Harrington.

" 'Scuze me, Mr. Harrington. I didn't mean to get in your way" he apologized even though it was the old man's hurry that had almost bowled him over. He was obviously aggravated and not in much mood to talk. Which, of course, he never was.

"Humph" was about all the undertaker could audibalize to go along with the nod of his head.

"Say, Mr. Harrington, you wouldn't be headed for home would you?"

"Yep, if that dumb Charlie will hurry up in the bathroom" he mumbled.

"My pickup quit on me, Mr. Harrington. And I sure do need to get home tonight. 'Spose you could give me a ride?" he ventured.

"I'm in the hearse." He said it in such a way Arch didn't know to take that as a yes or no. But the way he turned and headed into the parking lot, Arch took it as a "probably not".

"Mr. Harrington, I sure do need to get home tonight. And I don't mind riding in the hearse. I'll even be glad to help you drive if you'd like me to" he hurried along behind the older man.

"Got a dead man in there. You mind riding in back with the casket?" he offered.

"No sir. Don't mind it a bit. For a ride home I'd even ride in the casket myself." He chuckled. But the owner of the finest hearse in Oregon

28

wasn't going to ruin a well-earned reputation for solemnity. Not even a smile in the dark. He just muttered a "Hump" and opened the back door for Arch to climb in.

"Be sure and knock all that snow off your boots". Mr. Harrington hurried him along, motioning with one hand while he held the door handle with the other. "Just sit there, he pointed at the little jump seat by the front of the compartment.

The cold gray casket was strapped securely onto the sliding rails. A darkly tinted glass window separated the casket compartment from the front seat. Arch noticed that there was no handle on the inside of the door but then he didn't reckon too many folks riding in a casket needed a door handle. There was a sliding panel in the window to the front seat that did have a handle on it.

Arch stuffed his bag in front of the casket where it would not slide around on the narrow winding road between Pendleton and La Grande. The jump seat he squeezed into was small but it was comfortable enough. His knees were about as high as his chin. And since the seat faced the center of the hearse instead of forward, his knees were braced against the casket. He doubted that the occupant of this box would mind. And even if it were crowded and cramped, it sure beat standing out on the side of Highway 30 with your thumb stuck out on a cold night.

As he slammed the door, Meriwether swore. Where's that stupid Slingshot? Does it take him all night just to take a...?

"Hey, Mr. Mary-weather!" Slingshot shouted at the top of his lungs. Don't leave me. There was near panic in his voice as he ran for the hearse. "I thought you had left me. You scared me to death. I looked all over the place for you. You shouldnt have scared me like."

Almost to the hearse, Slingshot slipped on the snow and went sprawling. He was almost under the high slung pickup truck parked nest to the Cadillac by the time he quit skidding. He just glared at him and as if on second thought he turned and barked, "Get up and lets go", as he dug the keys out of his pocket. He pulled Slingshot by the arm and said Get that snow off your butt before you get in my hearse! He even made a swipe or two at brushing the snow off Slingshots back.

"You drive! was all he said as he pushed him toward the drivers door. It was completely within character for him to neglect asking if Slingshot had hurt himself when he fell. And with the confusing interruption it did not even occur to tell Slingshot about Arch in the back of the hearse either. That is, if he ever intended to tell him at all.

As Slingshot turned the key the big beast of an engine roared to life. He reached for the knob on the radio and Harrington immediately turned it off with a scowl. "And you better pay attention and be careful". The ice in his tone was as cold as the weather." He hated the way Charlie pronounced his name like it was two words.

"Yes sir, Mr. Mary-weather. I shore will. I'm always as careful as I can be with this here hearse. I know it cost you lots of money and I shore don't want to do nothin' to mess it up. I'll be extra easy with this here Caddy-lack tonight. You reckon they got the road ploughed and sanded pretty good by now? I know they git to work on it as soon as it starts snowing. They do a good job on it too, don't they Mr. Mary-weather?

The snow continued to fall lightly as they headed south. Fortunately, the ploughs had already been on the job and the packed snow base was well sanded. The old man had abruptly cut off Charlies excited monologue that he knew would continue until he did. Just shut up and pay attention to your driving he growled as he stared ahead.

As they cruised along the relatively flat road out of Pendleton, Arch drained the last lukewarm dregs of Maxwell House from his thermos and sipped it in darkness. By the time the thin plastic cup was empty, the gentle sway of the big Caddy and the hum of the wheels had almost rocked him to sleep. When he realized that the front end of the hearse was noticeably higher than the taillights, he knew they had begun the steep climb up Deadmans Pass. As the irony of it struck him he almost chuckled at the thought of his situation. Who would ever have thought that this dark October night, or any night for that matter, would find him headed for home, going buck hunting in a big black hearse! To be delivered to his own home in a chauffer-driven Cadillac! Man this was living! This college life was getting better all the time.

Arch managed to stay warm only as long as the coffee in his thermos held out. He had nursed his last cup until they had just passed the mid-way point up the long climb to the top of Cabbage Hill. The closer they approached the summit, the heavy hearse seemed to make slower and slower progress as Slingshot tried to keep up the speed without spinning out on the packed snow. And the longer they traveled, the colder it got in the back of the big wagon where Arch hugged himself and tried not to shiver so uncontrollably. By now the bone-chilling cold had pierced the outer layers of his coat, jacket and shirt and was beginning to penetrate his long underwear. Guess they never realized how cold it can get back here when they built these things he mused to himself. Then he almost chuckled out loud as at the thought of how uselessness a heater would be for the usual occupants of this compartment. He endured it about as long as he could when he finally determined he could stand it no longer. Maybe there were some of those grass-looking rugs they used around the graves in here. They might help hold off frostbite if he could find some and wrap them around his boots. But searching around under the casket proved fruitless.

When he could suffer it no longer, he pulled back the curtain that separated him from the passengers compartment, intending to tap on the glass and ask for relief. He hoped that the sliding window was not locked. Only then did he realize it was actually a good, wide window that would let thru plenty of heat.

What luck! He was sure that Mr. Harrington would not mind him opening it and allowing some of the warmth from the heater to preserve his life. Unfortunately, the man of few words had failed to inform his driver that there was a live passenger in the back of the hearse along with the silent one back with the casket.

Arch slid the window open and said "I'm freezing back here, Mr. Harrington. May I…"

He never finished the request. The terrified driver threw open his door and screamed as he bailed out. Fortunately, the hearse had slowed almost to a crawl, which was probably the only thing that saved Slingshots life and Meriwethers hearse. As he grabbed the wheel and attempted to scramble over into the drivers seat, the hearse chugged to a stop in the soft piled snow at the edge of the road.

Slingshot tumbled like a bowling pin when he hit the snow. Somehow he managed to come to up on his feet and headed back for Pendleton, slipping, sliding and skidding but whimpering frantically as he rapidly retreated down the hill. As he disappeared in the dark, both Arch and Meriwether jumped out of the hearse.

"Come back here, you idiot!" Meriwether yelled in the direction his hired help had vanished. But now there was no sound except the quiet purr of the big Cadillacs engine. "Humph!" was the total extent of the undertakers response as he got back in under the wheel.

In spite of his best efforts to control himself, Arch was nearly doubled in laughter. The stern and disgusted older man barked, "If youre going home with me, get in!" As Arch jumped in, Meriwether backed the hearse out of the snow and back into the southbound lane.

"Arent we going back to get Charlie?" Arch asked in surprise.

"Humph! Probably couldn't catch him!" he retorted as he headed for home.

Harrington dropped Arch off in North Powder and drove on to Baker City alone. Arch walked the two blocks home and the next day both he and his Dad killed nice bucks.

Mr. Harrington's trip to Pendleton and the ensuing funeral netted him a handsome profit. Charlie never did ask to be paid for his trip. Harrington didn't mind because it just added to the net income of this particular funeral.

As for Charlie Outhouser? Well, he was not seen in Baker City for over two weeks. And he has not asked to work for Harringtons Progressive Funeral Home to this day. Most folks don't believe you could kill him, lock him in a casket and put him back in that big black Cadillac that he deserted on top of Cabbage Hill.

FRIENDS
DON'T LET FRIENDS
HUNT CHUKARS

"Can you tell me what's happened to Mick?" The sheer panic in Ruth's voice was enough to terrorize the telephone line.

"Yeah, we went chukar hunting," I answered.

"He passed out just inside the door. When he came to he was mumbling something about killing you in a method I don't even want to talk about" she declared. Now I knew Mick was hurting when I let him out at the door but he didn't seem to be that bad off.

"He looks like death warmed over," she continued. "We are going to take him to the hospital but the doctor does want to know what happened to him."

"We went chukar hunting," I told her again.

I should have known that wouldn't be enough information for a newly transplanted easterner. This was their first year in our wide, wonderful, chukar-hunting west. And that probably also explains why Mick was ready to just pick up and go at my first invitation. Well, some folks learn more slowly than others.

After the x-rays showed a broken rib, punctured lung and many lacerations and bruises, they finally got Mick some relief with a needle full of oblivion. There are people on the streets of every major city in the U.S. who would kill or die for as much dope as they had to give him to ease the pain. And what they gave to calm him down probably saved my life as well. He would have shot me if he could have. It would probably have been justifiable homicide!

Anyone who would take his fellow man on his first chukar hunt should be hanged. The only legal defense would be if he had been assured that a proper will was prepared, adequate life insurance paid, had an earned diploma from a military survival school and/or a certificate of eligibility from a licensed mountain climbing course. The potential widow should be thoroughly informed and required to sign a waiver of rights to sue.

As I sat by Mick's hospital bed I was reminded of my first chukar hunting trip just a few years previously…

I lay on the side of that wind swept ridge scared to death. It was one of those times when your first prayer is for the hasty return of Jesus. "If you are ever coming to this earth in my lifetime, Lord, please do it NOW. Preferably within the next few minutes before I loose what very little grip I have left and slide all the way to the bottom of Hell's Canyon!"

How quickly your consciousness can turn from prayer for your own survival to plans of hurt for your fellow man. My next thought was of murder. If I survived my first attempt at what I was told was "chukar hunting", Arch and Doc were dead men. Fellow members of this POLE CREEK RIDGE ROD, RIFLE AND REUBEN SANDWICH SOCIETY of which I had just become a full-fledged, dues paying, card carrying member. After the high and lofty ideals with which I had been led to believe was the normal and noble way that the members cared for each other, this was treachery of the worst sort.

Oh, I was far past that stage when I thought this was an extended form of tortuous initiation. I confess this was my first assessment of the noble "sport" they had told me was chukar hunting. After the first two hours of torture and seeing no living creature, I was willing to struggle back to the Blazer (if I could find it) and admit that I had been had. This greenhorn sucker would humble himself and bear the shame of having been taken on the grown-up western version of a snipe hunt; also known in some sections of the nation as a wild goose chase.

But then I heard in the distance the faint and muffled boom of a gun and thru the mist of the cloud that hung over this ridge I saw what looked for all the world like Arch and Doc. They were actually shooting and then walking out a distance, bending over and it looked like they were putting something in their sack. At that distance I could not tell and my first thought was that they were really going

34

to great lengths to carry out this ruse.

When the realization dawned on me, there was that sick feeling in the pit of my stomach. But I saw it. Arch actually shot his gun. Anyone who will leave a blood trail of a wounded deer and spend 20 minutes scratching thru buck brush to find his empty brass ain't the kind of hunter who will just be shooting his gun to play a prank on a preacher. There must actually be a bird called a chukar!

I had long since given up on the hope that I was lost and therefore my fellow members would soon be searching and finding me. There was that exhilarating rush of excitement known only to combat soldiers pinned behind the enemy lines when the cavalry rushes in to take up their defense. It came with the roar of the rotors on the rescue 'chopper. They had found me and soon some daring hero would be descending on a cable with a thermos of hot coffee and winch me to safety. After the warmth of the hospital where they always take freed hostages, and a few days of recovery I would find my former friends and gladly shoot both of them.

My hopes rose as the roar got louder signaling the approaching end of my ordeal. But as the engine noise began to diminish the awful devastating reality crushed my spirits. Thru eyes blurred with tears I watched the single engine fixed-wing aircraft fly - *below* me. It was one of those planes in which they take sightseers to view Hells Canyon. From my precarious perch far above the ride of these rich and comfortable tourists, I remembered that these chukars were imported from the breed living as high as 16,000 feet up in the Himalayas. The pilot flying below me was probably on oxygen!

As I lay there far above the tree line I seriously considered suicide. My mind, numbed by cold and exhaustion, struggled to find a reason not to shoot myself and end this misery. As the cloud began to drop freezing rain in my face I began to have a strange feeling approaching warmth as my imagination began to conjure up the method by which I would mutilate the sadists who had tricked me into hunting on Hara-kari Hill. Shooting them would be too quick and easy. They had to suffer. I would begin by pouring molasses into the gas tank of Arch's beloved Blazer. Then I would carve "Thou shalt love thy neighbor!" in sarcastic 6-inch letters on the hood and paint a bull's eye on the tailgate. This should sufficiently enrage him to distract his attention from the tacks dipped in slow acting poison I would embed in the upholstery.

For Doc I planned a particularly painful and agonizing death suitable to a man in his profession. I would steal some of the stationery from his office and write a letter to the editor of the *Dummycrat-Herald* newspaper confessing that I had another wife in Pocatello and another whole family on the Colville reservation. I would also admit that I had bought my license to practice from a mail order house in California and that I was leaving town and anyone who owed me money should either forget it or donate it to the Society for the Prevention of Cruelty to Animals. Then of course, I won't even be accused of the murder. His wife Bessie, who is quite a trap shooter herself, will slowly and painfully strangle him with a pair of panty hose.

But somehow, neither of these seemed sufficient suffering for the agony I was enduring. As I struggled to think of an even more humiliating and excruciating form of homicide for my tormentors, I began to ask myself why they had been able to lure me into this in the first place. Then the disturbing question crept into my consciousness as to whether I must bare some of the blame. And if so I should shoot myself! -in the foot so I would slowly bleed to death. Was it because of some failure of my own which had brought me to the brink of eternity to die out here alone? All for the chance to shoot at some overgrown quail?

QUAIL! That's it. These chukar are nothing but another breed of quail. I guess I had heard that information before but it hadn't registered. At least not in my conscious mind. But my subconscious memory must have picked it up and there was no way the club was going chukar hunting without me even if I had to skip Sunday School to go. I have a score to settle with quail that dates back to that Thanksgiving morning in a Georgia swamp in my youth. (Ill tell you about that later.)

How I got home from my first chukar hunt is still a blur in my memory caused by a lack of oxygen, extreme fatigue and excruciating pain. The last thing I remember was struggling back in the direction of where I thought the Blazer was parked. My only motivation was

36

murder.

When Arch and Doc found me there were too many of them to shoot. I saw at least 3 or 4 of each of them. I think I would have still tried if I hadn't lost my shotgun! Fortunately the recovery period was of sufficient length that Arch and Doc had time to appease my wrath before my strength returned.

I was brought back to the present realities by the painful moaning of my most recent chukar hunting buddy. I was not sure that I was ready for him to regain con consciousness without a nurse in the room to protect me.

If I am lucky, Mick's wrath will be tempered by mercy before they take the body cast off. But I still have to face the woman who almost became a rich widow just because I took her husband chukar hunting!

QUAIL MONSTERS AND SNOT BUBBLES

Have you ever noticed how chukar hunters always run in packs? I mean you never see just one or two of them at a time like you do deer or rabbit hunters. They are not even like duck hunters of two or three to a blind. There are several reasons for this.

One of the main reasons that men only go chukar hunting with a crowd is the territory they have to hunt in. Chasing a wounded bear with a stick is not nearly as dangerous as hunting these helpless look-ing one-pound birds. Their defense is the remote, hostile and rugged terrain they inhabit. Every hunter goes with the nagging suspicion that this will be the hunt he won't survive. His only consolation is that there will be enough fellow-hunters to help carry out his carcass. You know that misery loves company. That saying probably originated to describe chukar hunters since it best describes the first charac-teristic of their hunting patterns. It is the real reason insane folks hunt chukars in gangs. Besides being totally void of any semblance of sanity, these crazy folks seem to enjoy sharing their misery with men of like mindlessness. I had always thought duck hunting was the most miserable fun I ever had. That was until I went on my first eastern Oregon chukar hunt.

My wife is convinced that the only reason I continue to go chasing chukars is to verify to myself that it isn't as bad as I first thought. But it always is… and worse!

The real reason I continue to try to kill those F-14s of the bird family is that I have a score to settle. If they were not just another breed of quail I'd have quit immediately after my first -which almost became my last- trip. But I'm still trying to get even. And it was all Buddy's fault.

His real name is Nathaniel Toliver but nobody called him anything but Buddy. He is one of the nicest and most likable fellows you'll ever meet, which is one reason he was always one of my favorite cousins. I never could figure out how a kid as kind and good as he was could make all-conference playing as an interior lineman. But he was tough and there were some pretty good high school athletes whose career came to a bone-jarring halt when they tried to encroach into the section of turf the coach told Buddy to protect. But that wasn't because he wanted to hurt anyone. He just took seriously his responsibility to defend the honor of Chattahoochee High School. I never knew Buddy to say an ugly thing about anybody nor to do anything but good to others.

Until he introduced me to quail hunting.

The greatest days of my life as a boy were the ones when we went to visit the Parkman's in that corner of north Florida where it meets Georgia and Alabama. They had a farm just across the line into Georgia and I must have been at least 10 or 12 years old. Tol, Buddy's daddy, worked in the egg business to try to make enough money to be able to farm for a living. He'd drive a truck all the way from Two Egg to Sawdust (both in Jackson County, Florida). On his route of buying eggs and selling feed, he got to know every farmer in the county. Which meant he also knew where just about every covey of bobwhite quail were located, too. He always carried a beat up old 16-gague shotgun in his truck and often came home with about as many dove and quail as he did hen eggs.

And he always had a tall tale to tell. One time I remember Tol coming home with a sack full of dove. It was dangerously close to the legal limit if in fact he hadn't exceeded it by a few. Buddy didn't think he had taken enough shells to warrant his having so many birds. Tol didn't have but one eye but it was his shooting eye and it was a good one. He didn't often miss. But when we were helping unload the truck, we found the whole box of shells unused. We knew then that someone had paid for their feed with birds instead of eggs.

But not so. Or at least Tol said we figured wrong. He said he had gotten up to Mr. Abner Dickinson's place and as he swung into the yard he noticed the old sagging power lines going from the back of the barn to the pole were loaded with doves. He asked Mrs. Dickinson if he could go shoot one or two and she said O. K. As he slipped around the corner of the building and raised the gun to shoot, it spooked the birds. When they all took off at once they knocked the two wires together and electrocuted 37 of the fattest doves in Jackson County. The other 4 died of pure fright, he claimed, which meant all 41 died from one form of shock or the other.

That night we lay in bed discussing the possibilities of there being any truth in the story. Our unanimous conclusion was that Tol had really told us a good one. Now, Tol is as honest as ole Abe and no man, woman nor child could ever accuse him of anything but above-board and fair dealing. But we never knew when he began one of his fishing or hunting stories just how much of it was true as it actually happened and how much was true as he actually remembered it.

At any rate, Buddy figured as how since this great hunting skill ran in the family, there would probably have been at least 60 or more dead doves if he had been there with his new Daisy Red Ryder B B gun. Why, with that new weapon he had already cleaned out the woods for a mile around the place. He had been personally responsible for the death of untold numbers of terribly poisonous snakes -some so big Betty Jo would have fainted if he'd even brought the dead thing to the house for the hogs to eat.

The more he talked about the firepower of that new gun and his skill with it the more fascinated cousin Bo and I became. But when it got to a certain point beyond credibility we just had to call him on it. His abilities were getting close to those of Daniel Boone himself. But Buddy declared it had a lot to do with that pretty new B B gun. We could probably even kill something with it ourselves. And tomorrow he'd prove it.

I don't know how long it took Bo to get to sleep. I didn't think I did but when Olene came to wake us up she didn't have to call twice. We were so excited we could hardly get our hunting clothes on. In fact, I couldn't. I didn't have anything but a brand new pair of Sunday-go-to-meeting corduroy britches. And besides, Olene said, we didn't have time to go hunting today. It was Thanksgiving and we had to go to Uncle Stanley's for the family reunion. We'd just have to wait to try out the new gun.

Now the most cruel thing that could happen to three mighty hunters approaching their teens would be get them all excited about a hunting trip and then tell them they couldn't go. And to make them get dressed up in church clothes and wait two hours was adding insult to injury. So we decided we could slip the gun out the window and wait till we were away from the house to load it. B B's in a gun make too much noise when you have to get past a fussy Mother and a sister who may tattletale on you.

We could slip over the back fence and be into the woods before anyone could see us. And a couple of hours was plenty of time for us to kill any wild game dumb enough not to have left the county when word got around that Buddy Parkman had a new Daisy Red Ryder. Between the 3 of us, we would probably kill enough fresh meat to feed the entire family reunion and have leftovers to take to the preacher. And there was plenty of game to shoot. These woods were full of squirrels, rabbits, 'coons, 'possums, wild boars and black bears. Just because nobody had ever seen some of them didn't change the fact of their existence.

We weren't into the woods 5 minutes before we heard our first victim. Unable to see our quarry, we crept down the trail just like they did in the movies. When we stopped hearing him, I assured my partners that it would be safer if they remained hidden while I -being the oldest- took the gun to make the first kill.

A decision I regret to this day.

I hadn't gone 50 yards down the path when that monster that had been lying in wait, attacked me with such vicious fury I didn't have a chance to get off a shot. He was black and ugly and I have since calculated his weight to be in the neighborhood of 600 to 700 pounds. His big blood-shot eyes glared at me with vengeance and snot bubbles spewed from his flared nostrils. He drooled in anticipation of sinking those 8-inch tusks into my flesh. As I fled from the beast his hot breath nearly scorched my neck and the stink of it still gags me to remember.

I honestly don't recall passing Bo and Buddy. I assumed that they had seen my peril and gone for help. No matter how loud I yelled they didn't come to my rescue. And my blood-curdling scream only made the monster madder and more determined to tear me limb from limb. As he bore down on me I summoned every bit of energy to outrun him, but it was no use. He had me.

I didn't feel a thing. I just couldn't move. I was lying on my back, panting for breath and this time I was the one blowing snot bubbles. I was afraid to open my eyes. And I didn't have to. The vision of that swamp monster is burned into my memory to this day. He must be eating me alive! As feeling began to come back I realized he has amputated my right leg and was holding me in his powerful claws while he slowly enjoyed the flavor of my blood. The horrible sound he was making convinced me this crossbreed is somehow related to the hyena.

When I could stand the pain no longer, I forced my eyes open. Mercifully and mysteriously the vicious creature from the swamp was gone. But I still couldn't move and that sound grew even louder. Then I realized the beast had tied me securely with barbed wire, planning to come back and continue his meal. He was probably tearing into Buddy or Bo or maybe he has even attacked the house. I had to get free to go for help. But no matter how I struggled it was no use. A one-legged boy tied tightly with barbed wire was food in the 'fridge for this beast. And his hideous howling laugh assured me he was still near.

I managed to roll over a bit but what I was able to see from this new position sickened and terrified me even more. Both Bo and Buddy were writhing on the ground. The beast had somehow managed to disable them and left them convulsing and agonizing. And he must be somewhere near them for his giggling was now coming from their direction.

As I became more conscious, I realized something wasn't right about the whole scene. Bo managed to pull himself to his feet, leaned against a fence post momentarily before collapsing again— in laughter! Buddy was unable to get higher than his knees and when he looked at me he again rolled on the ground. I was lying there bleeding to death and these idiots were laughing! Buddy crawled over by me and by the greatest effort he managed to stop laughing long enough to ask "Are you hurt?"

HURT? He asks! I have just survived an attack by the Florida cousin of the Creature From the Black Lagoon and he asks if I'm hurt!

As they were unwrapping me from the barbed wire, Buddy declared that I had stepped into the biggest covey of quail he had ever seen. He even admitted that when they flushed, the roar nearly deafened him. All he could see was birds in every direction, his new B B gun go strait up in the air and me emerging from the launch site faster than he'd ever seen a white boy run. When I passed them, Buddy had tried to tackle me high while Bo hit me low. They failed to even slow me down. If it hadn't been for that barbed-wire fence I hit in full stride, they reckoned I'd have been in Tallahassee before I quit running.

My amputated leg turned out to be no more than a scratch at the knee. But my new britches were ripped good. Now, I'd rather go back and fight a real monster than have to tell my Mother I'd torn those new Sunday britches. Bo and Buddy thought I was crying because my leg was cut. I wasn't. I was scared to have to have to go home and show Mother those britches.

I will go to my grave with gratitude to God for Olene's skill as a seamstress. She did such a good job Mother never even noticed. But the thing I'll love Olene most for is that she never told my secret. (Mother didn't find out about it 'til she read the first draft of this!) To this day, Olene laughs at the memory of three mighty hunters coming back to the house one Thanksgiving morning with a crying boy who has fought a monster. And the laughs have been worth it!

I'll never forget my first bird hunt. From that day 'til this, I have had a personal score to settle with quail and I won't miss any chance to try to get even.

So far, the quail are still ahead!

OLENE'S FUNERAL

It was one of those indecisive days weather wise. The mid-morning sun reminded me of a kid poking and peeking around and over and thru the crowd to get a look at the passing parade. The golden globe couldn't seem to decide whether to persevere or give it up and hide for the rest of the day. The dark, heavy clouds could not seem to decide whether they wanted to disperse or deliver a downpour.

There was no indecisiveness in my heart, however. I took the first dirt road right at the west end of the Apalachicola River Bridge. Another quick right brought me back under the concrete span and within yards I was into the cypress swamp. Slipping along the muddy ruts and sloshing thru the pickup sized puddles was going to make a dirty vehicle for a funeral procession. But I thought Olene would understand. And I knew she would approve.

Driving thru a swamp might seem a strange place to begin a day set aside for funeral and burial. But I needed the sanctuary of the swamp before the auditorium of the church to remember a good woman.

Realizing the time for the service was soon approaching I found a place barely wide enough for 4 or 5 back-and-forths to get my truck headed to town. I met the Toyota pickup as I got near the exit from the solitude. The brand new dog box in the back was in shiny contrast to the well-worn pickup. We paused in passing and lowered the windows to howdy but the driver just stared at me. I guess he wasn't expecting to see a fellow dressed like a preacher-going-to-meeting, driving a muddy F150 down in his coon hunting woods.

"You from these parts?" I asked.

"All my life", he hesitated to report. The suspicion was obvious on his face and mistrust in his voice. A stream of brown tobacco juice bulls-eyed the narrow spot between our trucks.

"I used to come down here with my kinfolks when I was a kid", I said. "You know about the Blue Hole?"

With the mention of that familiar piece of real estate, I could see the doubts begin to fade. Maybe this city slicker looking dude wasn't such a nut after all.

"Yeah. Hits back over yonder", he said. "Kinda hard to find. I don't think you could get there nohow". I wasn't sure if he doubted my 2-wheel drive Ford or my personal abilities. "Real hard to find", he added.

"Yeah, I member."

And that's why I was there. Remembering.

Buddy had a friend (seems like it was James Reynolds) who knew about this hot fishing hole that was loaded with monster sized bream, bass, crappies, stump knockers and Lord only knew what else. The fish were so hungry that if you didn't hurry and get your hook in the water theyd flop out on the bank, knock over your bait can and eat the worms. This honey-hole was the place where legends were made. The only reason *Field and Stream* hadn't been down here to write about it was that it was such a closely guarded secret. But James knew about it because one of his uncles had snuck him in one time.

You can imagine the compelling urge that overwhelmed us boys. We had the bait, we had the tackle, we had the time but we didn't have the transportation. This place was across the river and we were a couple of years short of a drivers license.

"Maybe Mama will take us," Buddy said.

It had never occurred to me that the mother of teenagers had the time, much less the inclination to go fishing with a bunch of boys. And I never thought that Olene loved fishing that much. But that day she demonstrated that she sure loved boys!

"Sounds like a good idea to me. Lets go." My surprise nearly turned to shock when I realized that she was actually going fishing with us. Not just delivering and picking us up.

Tol drove the truck to work so Olene had to take the family car. She parked it at the edge of the swamp and we unloaded our tackle, bait, snacks and lunch. James said it didn't matter anyhow; this Blue Hole was so remote wed have to walk. If walking is what you call sloshing and slogging and slipping and sliding and climbing over logs and jumping from one cypress knee to the next, we walked for what seemed like forever. We looked over here, back yonder, out there and into every mile of what must have been the biggest swamp in Florida. All to no avail. You couldn't prove by us that there was any Blue Hole in this black water swamp. Buddy even climbed a vine tangle up a tree to see if he could spot it.

The good-natured ribbing that James was getting became frustrated accusations that he had really pulled a good one on us. This wild fish chase was a wet snipe hunt we were getting real tired of. It was approaching pure ridicule when Olene finally stepped in and saved James life. I'm pretty sure that Bubby and I would have drowned him then and there if it werent for Olene's obvious amusement in this little excursion.

Despite our allegations, James still insisted that he wasn't joking. There really was a good fishing hole out here, somewhere. I think Olene purely enjoyed the fact that James had so fooled us into thinking that there really was a fish laden pond. She was caught in a world-class hoax and it was worth it to her to watch the misery of a couple of boys who were too eager to fish. Our youthful enthusiasm had made us easy to be fooled.

I wasn't really looking for the Blue Hole today. After all, it only existed in James joke. I just wanted to remember. And I wanted to go back to the swamp where Olene Parkman loved a place into the heart of this nephew. And I wanted to remember how she enjoyed teasing us for days about being so effectively bamboozled.

I don't know if Buddy or Olene ever found out for sure that there really is a Blue Hole in that swamp. I didn't find out until I met a coon hunter in a Toyota pickup.

I think there was a big grin on Olenes face -if she noticed- this boy in an old mans body a few miles west of the church where we would soon gather for her funeral.

A FILE
BY ANOTHER NAME...
MIGHT BE A FLAT BASTARD

What's in a name? That which we call a rose
By any other name would smell as sweet.
Romeo and Juliet. Act ii. Sc. 2.

The problem with all of us talking the English language (if you call what them yankees speak 'English'), is that we *assume* that we know what the other fellow said just because we recognize the words. That is a basic erroneous assumption that can mean more than just mis-understanding and confusion. It can prove downright embarrassing and sometimes it can be a total disaster.

I'm not talking about the technical differences in the use of termi-nology as regards unique fields. When the doctor talks about a faulty disk, you can check your insurance and get ready for back surgery. But a computer programmer's faulty disk means a 98-cent piece of floppy plastic.

If Raley Construction Co. buys a cat you know Larry has a new bulldozer. But his wife's new cat would more likely be a Siamese.

Serious problems were barely avoided early in our marriage when my wife finally taught me the difference between going shopping and going shopping. When she said she was going to the mall to shop, I naturally assumed she had something that she needed to buy. When she arrived back home hours later, feet sore and not one package to prove a purchase, I would get more than a bit frustrated and wonder where she had really been. A feller just doesn't expect his new bride to flat-out lie to him. What was she hiding? It was too far from Christmas, birthday or anniversary for her to be sneak-ing around that way. What she actually had been doing instead of what she told me she was doing fertilized my imagination to a near disastrous point.

I remember throwing a particularly bad fit one evening when I was tired and hungry. I had a long day bass fishing on Lake Martin near Kawliga beach and the wooden Indian. When she finally got home later than I did, I proceeded to lecture her on the wife's duties to be home with a warm supper and tender loving care for a husband who had worked so long and hard to try and put fresh meat on the table. Then she tried that "I've been shopping!" line on me. I hit the ceiling and accused her of lying. She had no evidence that she had even been near a mall. There were no packages, no sales slips, no charge card receipts and no other tangible evidence to serve as an alibi.

"Have you cleaned your fish yet?" she interrupted my lecture.

"I don't have any fish to clean!" I answered. "Didn't even get a good strike." But before I could get back to the subject at hand I got a strike. Harriet struck.

"How do I know you have really been fishing?"

Now, I may be slow but I ain't dumb. I was just slow enough to get myself caught tight in the very trap I had baited. And 40 years of marriage has not freed me from being reminded of it from time to time. There is as much difference in going fishing and catching fish there is in going shopping and buying something.

Difference in terminology in that case was just uncomfortable. At a beautiful secluded spot on Greenhorn Mountain it was near disastrous.

The POLE CREEK RIDGE GANG had just enjoyed a delicious steak lunch grilled over an open bed of coals. Big ole' juicy Walla Walla sweet onions and Idaho potatoes had been baked, 2 whole heads of lettuce with Tomatoes, radishes and carrots from Arch's garden had made the salad. A gallon of Harriet's southern style iced tea washed it all down. Every one was too stuffed to take on Peg Leg's apple pie just then.

Nellie stretched out on the grass and was soon snoring in the warm October sun. While Arch took out a clean rag and began to dust the inside of his precious Blazer, I wandered off across a small meadow

48

to look for deer signs. The women headed for the ruins of the old log cabin down by the creek.

It must have been an hour later when I got back, having circled around the meadow and coming out of the trees just below ole' Blaze. Nellie was struggling to get to his feet and the look on his face puzzled me.

The expression on Arch's face was one of rage turned to hopeless frustration. The pile of rusty metal junk on the tailgate attested to the fact that the women had found "treasure" and had infuriated Arch by putting the dirty junk in his newly cleaned rig.

Murder! Pure, meditated, calculated, mutilating mayhem glared from Peg Leg's eyes. She looked mad enough to eat Arch alive. I wondered if I was going to need to physically restrain her. Before I could say anything she screamed "Don't you dare call my friend such a name!" My Harriet had collapsed in an uncontrollable laughing seizure that threatened to take her breath. I didn't have a clue what was going on.

"I can't believe it. My own husband calling my very best friend such a name. She is *not* fat! And using a filthy word like that!" she squalled.

"I didn't say fat, I said *flat!*" Arch protested but with little success. By now I was totally confused. What in the world was this all about?

He looked to me with the desperation of an innocent deacon accused of the worst sin. Holding up a rusty and dirt covered piece of metal, the urgent begging in his voice was almost pitiful as he asked me "Do you know what this is?"

"It looks like a flat bastard to me. But with so much rust, it is hard to tell."

Arch dropped the file and gave me a bear hug that nearly cut off circulation. I think he barely restrained himself from giving me a big kiss! It has been a long time since I've seen a grown man so happy. And so relived.

"I was scared to death that a preacher would not even know a flat file from a hacksaw blade."

But instead of rescuing Arch from his predicament, I had just managed to put myself right into the middle of it. Peg Leg looked at me with sheer unbelief. Besides this preacher's surprising speech and her own husband's language, his erratic, bear-hugging behavior was too confusing for her comprehension.

Nellie was awake enough by now to have caught on to the mess we had gotten ourselves into. But instead of coming to our rescue, he just laughed. He was thoroughly enjoying our futile attempts to persuade her that a "bastard" was a legal name for the shape of a file. Among Peg Leg's weeping, Harriet's giggling, Arch's exasperated attempts at explanation and my embarrassed mumbling protests, Nellie finally spoke up.

"Check the dictionary. American pattern files are designated as coarse, bastard, second cut and smooth", Nellie explained.

As we sat around the table back in camp that night, Peg Leg's world-class apple pie was just as delicious as usual. Harriet still broke out in a giggle every now and then. Right in the middle of a conversation on any other subject that hunters normally discuss over the last cup of coffee in deer camp, Peg Leg would break in with "I still don't believe you. A preacher and a deacon talking like that!"

Our problem really wasn't settled until we got back to town at the end of deer season. Ole' Blaze took us directly to Maxi Mart Center. In the hand tool section of the hardware store there was a hastily called meeting of the POLE CREEK RIDGE GANG. It was there that Black and Decker finally settled the question for us once and for all. In bold black letters on a yellow package containing a brand new file was stamped "FLAT BASTARD"!

WHY CAN'T WOMEN GET MARRIED WITHOUT A WEDDING?

A NEW YEARS LETTER

Dear Charlie,

Contrary to what you have every right to believe, we are still listed among the living. I had fully intended to be caught up on all my correspondence by the end of the year. With the last dying strains of "Auld Lang Syne" I gave up and started the new year off clean.

By that I mean I just declared myself absolved of any responsibility to be a decent friend and communicate with any past due correspondence.

Beginning the brand new year with no friends doesn't strike me as a good way to launch into the first year of the rest of my life, so I repented and started all over again. Now maybe I'll at least have some friends, but the year is only eight days old and I'm seven days behind.

Not only is the mercy of the Lord new every morning, but in this new year He has seen my plight and intervened.

We have been experiencing the most snowfall in the Pacific Northwest since back in the fifties. There has been a sufficient amount of the white stuff to spread around all over the place and to a depth adequate to the cancellation of just enough travel as to postpone my scheduled meetings for the first two weekends of the year. Now, how's that for the Lord telling a fellow to stay at home and get caught up on his correspondence?

When you think of it, this is a much better deal than the Apostle received. When Paul got behind in his letter writing, the Lord threw him in jail until he got caught up. I am determined not to get that

51

far behind.

But I have encountered something of a problem this weekend. One of the young couples here is determined to get married.

Now, I think that is fine. In fact, I most highly recommend this glorious and delicious state of matrimony. It's all the silly foolishness the womenfolk are dead set on putting us thru to get into the status of "married" that I fret over. Weddings are a bore! An extravagant waste of money, man-hours and most of all, time. I never wanted to go to a wedding in my life, with the possible exception of my own.

And I emphasize possible. I didn't want to stand like a ridiculous stiff, dressed in a rented costume that looked more like a B-grade Yancey Derringer movie than sanity. Before a crowd of folks, most of whom were only there because their mother or their wife made them attend. But I did. And we have pictures to prove it. They are in that big white funeral looking book that we take out occasionally.

Actually, I should qualify that "we" — our children take it out every once in a while when they want to show some of their friends how funny people looked in the "olden days".

Yes, I did it. I went thru a wedding and actually took part in the thing.

Why?

Well, I was young at the time and very foolish. I had not come to the maturity of years to know that a man should stand up and be a man, should be willing to speak out against the foolishness and frivolity which our women bring up from their childhood, that a man should soar like an eagle, not perch like a parakeet.

But that's not the only reason I stood with that fatuitous flower in my lapel and allowed Dr. Lyon to ask me all those embarrassing questions. And all this before a deceptively sane looking crowd who were just waiting for a chance to act as daffy themselves by throwing rice all over me and my bride.

There was another reason. I was very much in love. I was infatuated with a Southern Beauty named Harriet Ann who had robbed me of my ability to think rationally.

What did I care if all my single buddies felt sorry for me. What if they came to the festivities only to laugh at the pitiful condition I had got myself tricked into. To show their contempt for their former companion, who was rudely and publicly deserting their ranks, they were defacing and probably dismantling my car.

But what did I care? I was in love! And at the time I thought she was worth a wedding. Well, that was over 40 years ago and time has proven my decision to have been correct. She was worth it. And you know what? She's even more worth it now.

But I'm still not going to that dumb wedding tomorrow. No, sir! My son and I will be miles away when they play that tiresome tune. We haven't decided just where we'll be yet but it won't be in church on Saturday afternoon. We could be snowmobiling. We don't have a snowmobile of our own but Dennis said we could borrow his anytime that he was not using it. And he won't be using it for a while. He's still in the hospital recovering from a broken pelvis he got the last time he used it.

Actually, we'd both rather go bird hunting. And I think we just might be able to go. I'm sufficiently recovered from our last chukar hunt the day before Christmas. The broken rib only hurts now when I sneeze.

I guess you have gathered by now that there's not much going on around here to write you about. No real news anyway. But at least when the folks around there ask if you remember me, you can tell them you heard from me one time in the new millennium.

Happy New Year, ole buddy,

Preacher

P.S. I went to the wedding after all. Harriet asked me to!

GRANT COUNTY MOUNTIE

The amount of time the television networks spend on a subject should reflect both the interest and importance of the issue or the personality. Usually, I guess, this is the case.

But in the past week we have been constantly bombarded with information and speculation about the death of actor John Belushi in a rented bungalow. He was a man who seemed to live by the motto "eat, drink and be merry." Even the networks reported him as being unrestrained in the self-gratification of his appetites. He was overweight, drank heavily and smoked excessively, they said. Now we learn his death was caused, at least in part, by drug overdose—self-inflicted abuse.

He was self-centered and loud. The image he often chose to portray was that of irreverence, sometimes bordering on sacrilege; arrogant non-conformity, risqu; vulgar. And I have the distinct impression that the death of John Belushi was far more important and interesting to the media than to the rest of us. I wonder if even his devout fans will maintain the sustained interest that news reporters give evidence of having.

And while they speculate and investigate, we here in Eastern Oregon mourn the death of a real man, a good man. He was a man who lived and died unnoticed by the mass media. He never drew a great income. He didn't own a fancy New England home and couldn't afford to rent a bungalow in Hollywood if he had been crazy enough to have wanted one. He lived and died in Granite. The media would report that "he lived and died in obscurity in Granite, Oregon." But the media didn't report. The media didn't even notice.

Most of the world doesn't even know where Granite is. (That's great to those of us who do.) But no one who has ever been near this relic of a town will soon forget our "Grant County Mountie." And we'll miss his deadpan "Yeah, this is Ringo" answer to our call on Channel 5 of our C B radio.

You see, he lived here by choice. And he lived in a near-ghost town for reasons other than honor or fame. He just seemed to love the place. Oh, neither the real estate nor the abandoned buildings. It was the people he cared about. And it was people he wanted to help. Someone needed to keep an eye on things when the owners left and went back to Baker and Boise. The Portland family could leave their snowmobiles in the shed. The Hermiston folks left their gold diggings with a flimsy chain across their road. Walla Walla weekenders left their cabins without undue concern.

Bud Morrow was on duty. And Bud was the law west of Blue Springs. The way Bud got his deputy star will give you an idea of the kind of man he was. It was about 20 years ago that folks began to notice, and appreciate, that Bud would keep an eye on their things just as if they were his own. So his friends and neighbors "deputized" him. The sheriff of Grant County later confirmed it.

Bud liked people. He liked to help people. He was soft-spoken and slow to get riled up—if he ever did. A simple southpaw who enjoyed visiting with the home folks as well as the outsiders who passed through.

It is disappointing that the national news media be taken up with the death of a self-indulgent play-actor while a gentle, giving man is murdered in the real world. But I don't care—and I feel sure that Bud wouldn't care—that they don't make a big deal of his death. Bud was no celebrity.

Or was he? What is a celebrity? If it takes riches and fame to rank, Bud did not qualify. If one has to have an inflated ego or a press agent, Bud is out. Flashy, he wasn't. Bud was no hero. But he was a good man. He was a friend, a good neighbor. You wouldn't think Bud had an enemy in the world.

But someone shot him. Cold-blooded and dirty. And that riles me. An honest and fair lawman was murdered. Some coward took the life of our friend. And I am more than a little concerned that his killer be caught, convicted and punished.

---

first published in the *Democrat Herald,* Baker City, OR

CHUNKIN' EGGS
AIN'T AGAINST THE LAW

One of my first responsibilities in life, I suppose you might even say it was my calling, is to make life as miserable as possible for my children. Considering I didn't even know I was expected to function in this capacity until just a few years ago, I must say that I have made remarkable progress. Probably due to my faithful dedication to, and practice in this much needed endeavor.

I first began to get suggestions as to my job when my son graduated from diapers. In fact, it may have been just a bit before that. Seems that before my firstborn learned any real words, he had a way of letting me know, and the whole world within earshot, that my ridiculous behavior was displeasing to him. Dumb things I did like forbid him to set his own bedtime. Or not allow him to drink out of the toilet or eat the dogs food.

About the time we began to get him house-broken, his little sister came along and reinforced his idea. She seemed to agree with him and proceeded to let me know in her own sweet little feminine way. And the older their mother and I got, the more unsatisfactory our behavior became. I think that the revelation was too slow in coming to me or maybe I was as dumb as they thought me to be. But one day McGooskie got tired of waiting for me to wise up. So he just flat out-told me, "You don't want me to have any fun!"

Did you ever have one of those slow-acting-type revelations hit you? It just kind of thuds into you at first and then begins to sorta sink in. You slowly start to realize that someone has put into words what you knew all the time in your sub-conscious. You just had not formulated it into a well-defined and articulated doctrine. When he said "No fun" it began to dawn on me. So I told him so.

It was a nice spring evening and I was preparing him for a particularly effective type of torture - weekly prayer meeting at the Baptist church. Everyone was ready but this 14 year-old unspiritual preacher's kid. And the protest he had mounted deserved press coverage.

"You never want me to have any fun!" he repeated.

"Well, Son, that word never covers a lot of time. Don't you suppose you are exaggerating?" I asked.

"No. You never want me to enjoy things everybody else does."

"Like what things?" I challenged.

But he was ready. Pulling a 5-month old shred of evidence from the tip of his memory he declared "Like Halloween."

"What about Halloween? We did have that back in October last year didn't we?"

"Yeah, but you wouldn't let me have fun like everybody in Baker did. Everybody but me!"

I probably should have taken him on to church gagged and hand-cuffed, but I didn't. Like I told you, something was dawning on me. So I sent my wife and the girls on and we continued this little discussion.

Now, I love to have fun just as much as anyone. In fact, some folks think I love fun a bit more than is reverent for a man whose professional title is "Reverend". So I was naturally interested in what kind of fun he had missed on Halloween. And more importantly, what kind of fun I had missed. It took no more than an opening for him to tell me all about it and to cite examples as proof of his point.

He was not allowed to throw eggs on Halloween night. Like everyone else did, of course. I proceeded to lecture him on the reasons why he could not participate. And he continued to tell me that throwing eggs on Halloween night was just harmless fun. My ace in the hole was the legality of the sport. He could be in trouble with the law if and when he got caught.

I should have known. His legal knowledge far surpassed my anti-quated notions and old-fashioned ideas. Egg throwing was not il-legal.

If the police did see you they would only ask you to stop he assured me. The extent of their disfavor would be no more than to simply ask you to throw all your remaining eggs on the ground in their presence. Under strict and close cross-examination, my legal expert assured me that I had cruelly denied him a night of no more than good, clean fun.

And since that was the case, I decided that making up for lost time was far more important than prayer meeting at this point. We had some fun to catch up on.

"Go get your jacket. I'll get the eggs," I instructed a very surprised teenager. He still didn't believe me when we were in the car and leaving the driveway. "Watch out for that city police car. I hope ole' Pierce is on duty tonight. We'll get him good and pay him back for giving your Mother that ticket last week."

"You aren't going to throw at him are you?" Goose asked. "I don't believe we can outrun him."

I explained that we wouldn't need to outrun him. Since it was just clean fun, Officer Pierce surely wouldn't mind. After all, he might even enjoy a little fun himself.

But Goose somehow didn't seem to think my suggestion was such a fun idea. As we cruised the streets looking for that blue car, he became more nervous. When I shouted, "There he is!" Goose nearly fainted even though it proved to be a false alarm. After several minutes of fruitless search, I complained that cops never could be found when you want one. Goose admitted he had gotten the point and was ready to give it up and head for home.

"Isn't this fun?" I laughed. Goose scowled. "Well, if they won't come out, we'll just go in and get them, I declared as we headed for City Hall.

Now he was beginning to squirm. "You really aren't going in there, it was hard to tell if it was a question or a demand as we pulled up to the front door of the police department. He was ready to beg. "This is ridiculous, he declared.

But it wasn't ridiculous to me. It was fun. And it was getting to be more fun all the time. I was afraid he was going to run when we got out. But he went inside because I threatened him with his life if he deserted me in our fun. Vowing to remain speechless, he declared he was only going inside to watch me make a fool of myself. I really was having fun. Why hadn't we done this before?

The sergeant was talking on the phone with his back to the door when we walked in. Glancing over his shoulder nonchalantly, he was not prepared for the scene. Into his office walked a smiling old man with both hands full of eggs obviously having fun and a scared teen-ager with a look of incredulity all over his face. When I rared back to throw an egg, the cop dropped his phone and Goose carefully grabbed my arm.

"What the devil are you doing?" the cop asked, not knowing whether to duck behind the desk or draw his pistol.

"I am having fun!" I emphatically and truthfully declared. "You don't mind if we have a little fun in here, do you?"

Before he could answer, Goose spoke up. By now he had taken all my eggs. "You see, my Dad and I were just talking about throwing eggs…uh…and…uh…I, uh…he said…uh…Well, is it against the law to throw eggs?"

Obviously the desk sergeant had slept thru the police academy lecture on how to handle being personally assaulted by an egg throwing old man and a reluctant assistant teenager. He was caught by such surprise that his answer sounded like he wasn't hitting on all cylinders.

"Well, actually…uh…the…uh…er… well, you can't…uh… I, mean it is not against the…uh.. . Well, it is…I mean…but

You know, this egg throwing was getting more fun all the time! I wondered why I hadn't tried it before.

The policeman began to recover sufficiently to give Goose a lecture on the evils of defacing public and personal property. Then he mumbled something about the dangers of hitting someone who might be bigger than you and thereby provoking a fight, which was against the law. I thanked him for his help and we left with Goose reluctantly protecting the eggs.

"Son, that WAS great fun. Thanks for letting me in on it" I said as we headed for home.

It was six weeks before Goose would even eat an egg for breakfast!

HOW NOT TO ROB
A GEORGIA BANK

"We could rob the Sumpter Bank!"

The Pole Creek Ridge Gang was lounging in the cabin, drinking coffee and finishing the remains of Josie's chocolate cake while we discussed the increase in the cost of Oregon's hunting licenses. It had been another successful day hunting mule deer. I should point out that this did not necessarily mean we had killed anything. Our exclusive society did not need bloody hands and dead meat to have a successful day in the mountains. Just being together in the Oregon outback - the best country in the country - made a day worth living and gave occasion for celebration with cake, coffee and cloth napkins.

That's when Nellie suggested a heist of the local repository of Sumpter's hoarded fortunes. It did not even merit a giggle out of the girls but it gave me an idea. "I think we could pull it off, I declared. "After all I have had some experience in that activity." I had their undivided, though unbelieving attention. Only because the statute of limitation has expired do I dare let you in on my brush with big-time crime.

As was our custom Friday night, Gerald, Reed and I met at the dorm after we had taken our dates home. But midnight was far too early for college men to give up a free weekend. As we contemplated some exciting way to get all the life into the hours before our Saturday night date, someone suggested that we go to Florida and back. If that would not impress a co-ed they were beyond impressibility. In those pre-interstate highway days, the distance from our college town to the Georgia/Florida state line was a matter of narrow two-lane roads thru farm country, small towns and big city of Valdosta. After much serious discussion and detailed planning which lasted 2 or 3 full minutes, we hit the road in the only available transportation—my 54 Chevy. Our total combined financial assets were a dollar and fifty-four cents. We purchased a dollar and fifty-one cents worth of gas and a piece of penny bubble gum for each of us. At my current rate of MPG we figured to drive 40 miles, park the car and hitch-hike to Florida and back from there. We would have reliable transportation on the first and last leg of our journey.

After long stretches of standing on a lonely Georgia road in the middle of the night, a soldier going home on leave picked us up and deposited us 50 miles further south. Then there was 30 or 40 miles in a truckload of chickens. The rest of the night and the variety of conveyances are a blur in my mind but I can still close my eyes, hold my nose and tell you what 5,000 chickens smell like on a sultry humid night. You'd gag if I told you.

Our goal was the Gulf of Mexico but by daylight we had not even gotten out of Georgia. So we concluded that if we could just get across the state line we could at least say that we had been to Florida. We were riding with a black preacher who was singing spirituals at the top of his voice when we crossed the line. We stopped the preacher between the verses of "Swing Low, Sweet Chariot" and got out a half mile inside the Sunshine State, crossed the road and headed back north.

If it was hard getting a ride in the middle of the night, the day light hours were only worse. As the sun grew hotter, we grew hungry and the passing drivers all became blind to our thumb. Finally a well-dressed man in a nice big Buick picked us up. I thought Gerald was going to hug his neck.

Scarcely had he gotten back up to the speed limit when he announced rather matter of factly, "I am going to rob the bank of Hahira!" With bold confidence he continued, "But I do need your help."

Of course, we didn't believe him. Until he began to unfold his plan. Since Gerald was studying for the ministry he could create an excellent distraction. He could start preaching on the street and divert attention from the rest of us. We would be able to empty the first state bank of the $686,429 dollars they currently had in cash. Gerald nervously told him that he left his Bible at school. Whereupon our chauffeur promptly produced a Gideon Bible, which he said, he had stolen from his motel room of the night before. Opening the glove compartment he showed us the '38 special that Gerald was to have in his pocket just in case we needed more immediately effective firepower than just a hell-fire sermon.

Our strategist then designated Reed as the wheelman and gave a detailed description of the location of the bank, the layout of the parking lot, the surrounding streets and the get-away route. We would plan to hit the bank at 11:00 A.M. while both local police would be at the station changing shifts. At least that's what he said.

He sure seemed to know a lot about this little town, the people, the police and the bank, which only increased our anxiety. But when he told me my part, my anxiety vanished and I was griped with sheer, cold panic. In the violin case on the seat beside me was a loaded Thompson sub-machine gun, he said. When he asked if I'd ever fired one, I lied and said no. Actually, a Chief Petty Officer stood me on the fantail of the U.S.S. Bowers and made me shoot at milk cartons bobbing in the Atlantic until I could hit one. So as Al Capone began to give me detailed instruction on the size, weight, feel and operational characteristics of the Tommy gun I knew that he knew exactly what he was talking about.

I was to accompany this desperado into the bank carrying the Tommy-gun in its case. We were to walk right in to the bank manager, whose name and description he supplied. Only then was I to pull the gun and emphasize the insistence of our request for an immediate withdrawal.

By this time, my mind was flashing "panic". I seriously contemplated bailing out of the car even though we were doing 60. Getting splattered all over a Georgia highway beat life imprisonment in the Atlanta penitentiary! I was sure if I jumped Gerald and Reed would go with me. Maybe I could pop the violin case open quick enough to get the Thompson pointed at this bank robbers head and stop the pending crime.

"The violin case is locked, but I'll give you the key before we get there." Now he was reading my mind! We'd had it, unless Gerald could grab the pistol from it's holster and stop the madness. The usual grin on Gerald's face was gone and there was a tear running down Reed's cheek. Would the law ever believe us?

By now I had given up hope of escape and begun to contemplate my bleak future. If I were lucky, the local cops, the Georgia State Patrol or the FBI would catch us soon. Dead or alive really didn't matter. My Daddy was going to kill me if the law didn't get me first. And to be honest, I preferred the criminal justice system to my Daddys. He was not limited by a Supreme Courts idea of what was cruel and unusual punishment.

Since there was no other hope I began to pray earnestly and silently. I repented of everything I could think of, even some things I had only thought about doing. In desperation I even promised God I'd study more and give up girls and football. This was serious! Maybe I wouldn't have to wear prison stripes after all. Maybe I'd get lucky and die full of bullet holes in a bloody shoot out.

As we neared Hahira the more panic-struck we all became. No one was talking now. Except this Baby Face Nelson who seemed to be enjoying it more and more as he rehearsed the details of the hit. When he asked us how we would spend our share of the loot, all I could think about was the home I'd never see again. I was so scared I couldn't even swallow my own spit. Reed struggled to hold back the tears and Gerald's nervous laugh was almost a giggle and he said, "You've got to be kidding!"

"The churches of Hahira welcome you", the sign said to everyone else who read it. What it said to me was "The Hahira jail welcomes you."

"Fellows this is going to be a piece of cake!" Machine Gun Kelly said. I couldn't tell if he was excited about the robbery or immensely enjoying seeing us so nervous.

As we approached Hahira, I spotted what I calculated to be my only chance to jump and run. There was a traffic light where we would probably have to stop. I prayed for red. In His mercy, God answered with what immediately became my favorite color.

Grasping the door handle, I was just ready to bail out when the man groaned, "Oh no, fellows. This is Saturday. The bank is closed today! We can't rob a closed bank." Reed could hold it no longer. He cried. Gerald shouted "Praise God!". I fainted.

Instead of robbing the Hahira bank, our chauffeur treated three hungry and much relieved college men to breakfast. He turned out to be a professor of banking at a Florida university. The president of the Hahira bank had been one of his former students. Our chauffer was a deacon in his church and active in the Gideons. In addition to playing practical jokes on college students he also played the violin.

I gave up bank robbing and swore off hitchhiking.

A SOUTHERN BELLE WHO WALKS ON WATER

There are a lot of fringe benefits to being married to your best friend. I had known this gal all her life. In fact, her mother was holding my mother's hand when I was born. She promised to go home and start a family. "Ill have a girl for him to marry", she promised. And true to her word, ten months and two days later she gave birth to her first and only daughter. That's good planning. But it's another story, too.

What I started telling you about were the fringe benefits. Like charm, beauty, brains, good personality, a great cook and the ability to walk on water.

She was elected Miss Congeniality in Robert E. Lee High School and a class beauty in the exclusive womens' finishing school where she went to college. Besides her degree, she earned a varsity letter in five sports. She was a gifted high school math teacher, but even though she never repented of that, she did quit, so I forgave her for that.

She is a pianist and an even better organist. She can sew beautifully, has taught swimming and life saving and a largemouth bass she caught on Lake Martin is still the family record.

How in the world a charming, elegant young lady like her ended up with a country bumpkin like me is a mystery worthy of Sherlock Holmes's attention. But her family's political connections did get me appointed to the staff of a very colorful Alabama governor. And her help, encouragement and inspiration got me through a couple of graduate schools.

The only thing this Southern Belle could not do when we married was cook. Her mama's maids had done that kind of work. She couldn't even boil water without scorching it or make toast without a detailed recipe. But I gladly declare that she HAS learned and today is the best cook in 50 states and all the provinces of Canada! If Colonel Sander could have fried chicken as good as my Harriet, he would have been a five-star general.

Our daughter gathered all her recipes together into a cookbook for her siblings and cousins for Christmas. She entitled it *Southern Belles Don't Have to Cook... But Mom Was a Preacher's Wife!*

Charm, grace, beauty, brains and ability she has it all. And I did tell you that she could even walk on water, didn't I?

Now, I did not actually see her do it. At least, I don't think I did. But there is no doubt in my mind that she did. And if she did not, she could have if she had thought it would have gotten her away any faster.

We were visiting missionary friends who were working two hours flight in a single engine airplane beyond civilization. It has been called the Green Hell of South America at the headwaters of the Amazon River in Bolivia. That far from the supermarket you depend on what you can catch, raise or shoot for your daily food. But it is like living in God's grocery store with the delicious tropical fruits and the abundance of fish and wildlife. And of all the gourmet delicacies in that jungle, alligator is by far the most delectable. Just the thought of Harriet's fried gator tail and cornmeal hushpuppies has me drooling in my keyboard now! Put just a dab of that on your forehead and your tongue would slap your brains out trying to rake it into you mouth.

Securing the main ingredient is the first step, of course. But getting my Southern belle, city gal in that little boat on a jungle river on a moonless night was probably the major feat of the trip. But she was the one who insisted on going. In addition to her other qualities, she has guts and grit.

Quietly paddling down the Hediondo River, we stopped from time to time and used a flashlight to search for red eyes looking back from the shallow water and the weeds along the bank. Those red eyes are just above and behind the most ferocious set of razor sharp teeth and are propelled with explosive speed, driven by a voracious appetite.

Harriet was holding the light and I had the gun while Wallace paddled. I wouldn't say Harriet was nervous but that flashlight covered more territory than the beacon at the Baker airport. She shined it all over every tree, up and down every vine, all over the boat, over, under and around every log and into everybodys eyes.

Our first gator was a nice little fellow about five feet or so. I blew away his whole mouth and half his face with a 12-gauge shotgun. Then Wallace put a .22 bullet in his brain for good measure before laying him across the boat just behind the seat where Harriet and Barbara were. Now she had something else to shine her light on and she checked every six seconds or less to make sure our breakfast was still dead.

The second one was a bit bigger and demanded that she check them on a much more frequent routine. She, of course, continued to keep a close check on all the surrounding jungle even though we did not need any more meat.

But then there he was! With eyes so far apart, he had to be the granddaddy whopper of the river. We paddled silently and carefully over toward him. This time the light didn't move. Harriet was frozen on this point like a well-trained Irish Setter. But while we watched, the eyes vanished, sinking our trophy silently beneath the deep dark water to safety. We were still a boat length or two from shore as we sat with baited breath hoping he would surface somewhere nearby.

The eerie soundlessness of midnight in the pitch-blackness could almost be felt. I was chilled in spite of the sweat trickling down my back. There was not even a ripple on the glassy surface of the slow moving river. The world seemed to be in a state of suspended animation.

That's when it happened. A fish about the size of my hand exploded from the depths and landed in Harriet's lap. She had released it so quickly I could swear that flashlight hung in midair. The fish was given the entire boat seat on which to do his frantic flopping.

I never saw her leave. The boat didn't even wiggle when she abandoned ship. There was not even a footprint, much less a ripple on the surface of the water. But somehow Harriet was on the bank of the river, jumping up and down screaming in what must have been a language she learned in that ladies college.

Like I said, I did not actually see her walk on the water. But that river was deep and her clothes weren't wet except for one spot. And if she had jumped that far at the Olympics they would have given her all three medals.

How and why she got back into that boat so quickly without dumping us all in the water is an equally mystifying question. Maybe you should ask her about that one.

LAND THAT I LOVE

We were sitting in church in that sprawling metropolis of McEwen, OR when Frank Snyder gave each one a piece of paper to record our answers to the quiz. We did not have to show anyone the answers for which I rejoice with relief. But, I will confess now to one of the questions and my answer.

"Is there anything you are afraid God will ask you to do if you give yourself wholeheartedly to anything He asks?" My immediate response was almost a reflex—"No, there is nothing I would not do for my Lord's sake."

He must have anticipated it because Frank then asked us to take more time and really search our heart. That's when the real answer came from deep within. It must have been there all along, hiding somewhere in the subconscious, woven deeply within my very being, gut-level deep. Stamped like a watermark on my soul is the compassionate love I have for this wonderful land of eastern Oregon.

Painfully, I had to admit that the only thing I really feared was that one day God would move me from this land I love. I will resist the temptation to begin to list all the reasons for my feeling this way. In fact, I am not sure what it means myself or where it all comes from. I have a nagging thought out there in the misty haze of subconscious of my understanding like a bull elk on a foggy morning. You smell him, hear him, and even feel him but you can't actually see him. No matter how hard you strain your eyes, how desperately you will yourself to perceive through the thick brush and icy fog. But he is there and you know it.

And somewhere out in that murky dimness of my cognizance it lurks. Winning the game of hide-and-seek, it plays with my fully conscious understanding. Yet it teases and torments me, giving just a fleeting glimpse here, the snap of a twig over there, movement in the bushes just beyond the focus of blurred vision. Why do I love this wonderful land so much and why do I dread to leave it?

Was it the childhood fantasy of a barefooted boy in Georgia who read too many cowboy comics? The theme song of the old Maverick TV series—what were those words? "Wild as the wind in Oregon, blowing up a canyon... I was just a teenager then. Vivid pictures in my mind from nearly 40 years ago of fascinating stories from the Oregon Trail in a third grade reading book.

No, not here. Surely these had something to do with the love affair I've had with this land for so many years. But it's not here. Where then? I have not found it yet. These memories are vivid and sharp, but there's something deeper and even more real. But where is it?

Wait a minute! There it is, hanging on my wall in plain view. It has been there all the time, but so well hidden by its conspicuousness. The fog begins to lift; is this really it?

She died when I was 17 years old. And every day of those first 17 years of my life she had prayed, "God make my grandson a preacher," or so I'm told by everyone of those ladies in her Sunday School class. And my godly grandmother never missed one of her Sunday School classes—or any other meeting of her church.

My heart broke when she died. I loved her so much and missed her. And when the family got together to sort out her things and sell her house, I asked them for something of hers. In fact, she had already promised it to me. Of all her worldly goods and because of her love for me, I think I could have asked for anything and had it—of all she owned I asked for one book and one picture.

Now it hangs on my wall, that one picture. It is not a painting and not even an expensive photograph or drawing. The paper is so thin it is even moth eaten in a spot on the corner. It looks like one of those flimsy pictures they use just to fill a frame before you buy it. But she hung it on her wall. And it has been there in my vivid sub-consciousness since before my conscious memory can recall.

The picture is a silhouette of an Indian standing against a big sky. He's on the top of a butte in a rocky outcropping. Really there's not much in that picture to look at. But it is what that picture "says" that has fired my imagination, fed my dreams and inspired my concept of just what the big, beautiful, wide, wonderful west is all about. It says freedom to stand on the precipice of a cliff you climbed all alone—to survey the vast expanse of beauty especially created by a God of infinite power—the quiet solitude afforded only by a place such as this where the only sound is the whisper of the wind in the pines or the cry of an occasional hawk.

This ancient photo says to me that there is a place in this country where one can actually feel the reality of David's Psalm: "Be still and know that I am God… I will be exalted in the earth!"

And one of those things for which I so dearly love this great land is just that. This very land itself, the mountains, deserts, rivers and waterfalls, majestic Ponderosa Pine and stately Douglas Fir, stubborn sagebrush and delicate fern; the deer, the antelope, elk, coyote, eagle, mountain trout and spawning salmon; multi-colored sunsets and wonderful scenes after a snow. This real estate itself declares the handiwork of a God of infinite variety and unsurpassed beauty. It speaks to me of a God who has created in beauty what He could have done in drabness.

There is no functional purpose for a sunset to contain a thousand shades of orange or purple, but it is beautiful. The infinite subtle varieties of green in a mountain springtime growth need not be there, but it is and it is beautiful. All trout could just as easily have been brown and all flowers smelled like alfalfa: all bucks could be forked horns and all the berries could taste like spinach. But they don't! And the only reason for most of the vast variety is just because God loves us and gives us these to enjoy.

I know of no place on this earth—and I've seen lots of it—nowhere does the handiwork of the Creator more glaringly nor more vividly declare the glory of God. And I love Him more because of it.

CHOPPIN' HIGH COTTON
OR
BRITISH HIGH TEA

It was obvious I was way out of my class when that big, brown Indian with the gold teeth and the uniform right out of the movie set opened the door for me. I hesitated a moment, wondering if we were at the right place until a quick wink and a grin from Calvin moved me. As the brass-buttoned and shoulder-padded uniform with the tasseled cap closed the car door behind me, another bowed, smiled and ushered us into the lavish lobby. The hush of elegant grandeur awed me as my Malaysian host directed us toward the imposing coolness of the Terrace Garden room. It was time for high tea in the Regent Hotel of Kuala Lumpur.

Through huge, carved wooden doors we stepped back two generations into the world of British colonialism. The immaculately tailored mai'tre d' smiled graciously as he bowed and delivered us into the care of a graceful hostess. With sparkling black eyes, dark complexion and raven colored hair, this miniature maiden was typical of those tiny Malaysian women known for their delicately featured beauty. Dressed in traditional sarong and bare feet, she ushered us thru plush Persian carpet to our seats. As we sank into the comfortable couch, I noticed the richness of the music and observed that it came from a polished, 9-foot concert grand piano played by a master dressed in formal tuxedo.

Around the large, low ceiling room were other couches and chairs, all arranged into a U-shape around low, hand-carved tables. Soft lighting and tastefully quiet music gave the feeling of cozy richness bordering on the extravagant. When our pianist took an occasional break from his Beethoven and Brahms, the soothing splash of the fountain added to the relaxed setting. Then she was back. Kneeling at our feet, she blended and steeped each person's tea and added the cream or sugar as directed. She left us with our expensive china plates and heavy silverware after directing us to the buffet table of delicacies. Someone once told me never try to impress anyone with the profundity of your thought by neither the obscurity of your speech nor the verbosity of your language. I'm not finished looking up all those 2-bit words, but somehow it seems to apply here. So I will not try to describe the overabundance of the grandiose table which those high-flouting' big shots called a "British High Tea". I'll just tell you flat out, I was choppin' some high cotton, as we'd say in Georgia! This country preacher from eastern Oregon was out of his class. But, boy was I faking it! As long as I could keep my eye on Calvin and do what he did, I was getting along pretty good.

As we sat listening to the little brown tux tickle the teeth of that over-sized Steinway, I remember asking myself "What am I doing here?" And when Calvin excused himself to go to the little boys' room I had a few moments of solitude to reflect on the reality of this situation. My next question was "Am I really here?" The thought crossed my mind that I had fallen asleep in the midst of an old black-and-white Bogart flick and was just dreaming. But even Ted Turner couldn't add this much "rosy romantic color" to an old film. It must be real and I must actually be in Asia, 12,000 miles from Pole Creek Ridge!

Being this far from home was nothing new to me. That is, the physical miles between here and the valley I love. But the two different worlds, which I had somehow managed to visit, were more than measurable miles apart. From the Regent to the Ridge! From the artificial elegance of polished furniture and potted plants to Ponderosa pine and pink sunsets. It was the difference between re-filtered air conditioning and a fresh mountain breeze. The difference between man-made sounds from piano wires and the music that only the Master Composer can make with a little bit of wind and a few pine needles. These two worlds were as separated as Persian carpet from a lodgepole patch.

One was manufactured while the other was created. And although they are both very real, the outdoor world of eastern Oregon is definitely the one in which I feel most comfortable. I don't mind visiting Malaysia and sipping high tea occasionally. But somehow I just never do really enjoy it like I think a fellow should. Regardless of how delicious the dainties or how tasty the tea, a part of my mind and all of my heart is off on a ridge somewhere in Baker County. There is a mug of strong coffee, a beautiful view and the sneaking suspicion that this is where the Lord stood when He made the rest of the world.

CLOSE CALLS

It seems to me it was an ad for some kind of pill for the cure of backache or maybe it was constipation. I remember they always had some very relieved looking old lady who ended the commercial with the statement that she felt just like she "had a new lease on life!"

It was that reprobate old Englishman who wrote the stories about a fantastic hero in the queen's service so super-duper he had to have a double O serial number. Frankly, I've never met an Englishman yet with half the guts or one-tenth the charm of that floozy chasing, sissy talking concoction of a boring British imagination.

But Ian Fleming entitled one of his books "You Only Live Twice". Any association with that book and the afore-mentioned problems that needed the advertised remedy is purely intentional. Thankfully, I don't remember enough about it to recall why he said you live twice but it seems like it had something to do with surviving some hairy scrape with certain death. He may have had a point there. I've escaped a few of those close calls that leave you feeling like you've been granted a second chance for some unknown reason.

I remember...

The little red and white Super Cub settled into the final approach with all the finesse and grace that Bill Piper designed it to do over 40 years ago. The STOL conversion added even more stability and permitted us to fly at an air speed as slow as 38 MPH. The windsock indicated a gentle breeze blowing across the runway from our left. Everything was normal, everything smooth on this beautiful sunny summer day. Without any warning, a strong maverick gust of wind bent on destruction assaulted us from the south and nearly flipped us onto our side. Jerking violently up on the left, we started what became a terrifying 360-degree turn with only the right landing gear touching the ground. I hung in the harnesses of the back seat watching the wing tip skim the freshly cut grass just inches from digging in. It happened so fast I hardly had time to pray. The fuel gages indicated over 1/2 full just before touch down. I knew that if the wing tip hit the ground we'd be cart wheeled into a bouncing, bloody, burning mess all over runway three-four of the Baker airport.

To this day, the pilot does not know how he managed to ride it out. We both kissed the asphalt and concluded that the Lord just spared our lives.

That was a close call!

A black ugly water moccasin won't grow much over 4 or 5 feet long. But what he lacks in size he makes up for in his dirty rotten attitude. He'll go out of his way to slither into your boat, drop from an overhanging tree into the middle of a peaceful, minding-your-own-business fisherman's lap. Or he'll deliberately enter your fish trap and wait all night and half the day for a chance to sink his deadly fangs into your hand. From the day before that first serpent allowed the Devil to use his lying lips, it has not been smart to trust a snake. And of all the breeds, varieties, shapes, sizes and types, the cottonmouth moccasin is the low-down dirtiest creature that God ever let live.

I could have been a famous man but at the time I had other things on my mind- survival being at the forefront. I read in the encyclopedia that the largest cottonmouth on record is 6 feet long. The one I met in a Louisiana swamp on a bass fishing trip was a Boone and Crockett, world class, record setting 40 feet long if he was an inch.

We had a nice string of fish and were headed for home. I laid my paddle behind me and reached for the log to pull us to the bank. My hand was within inches of tickling his tonsils, if moccasins have tonsils, when Charlie hollered, "SNAKE!" I didn't even see him at first but when I did I couldn't see anything else.

I fell backwards in the boat and the wetness in my britches wasn't from the water in the bait bucket which I sat in. Somehow I managed to get my pistol out of the tackle box and point it at the blackness on the bank. My hand was shaking so bad I had to try to hold steady by using both hands. I still don't know how I managed to shoot a hole in the bottom of my boat and miss my foot. And with a target as big as that moccasin, I don't know how I missed him. Charlie said my double nine revolver sounded like Elliot Ness' Tommy gun. Pop, pop, pop, pop, pop, pop, pop, pop, pop; and then about as many more clickety, clickety, clickety, clicks as I kept pulling the trigger on empty cylinders.

That wide-open cotton white mouth was as big as the bottom of dinner plate. With all my bullets spraying around him, I could have sworn that devil was laughing at me. He closed his mouth into a leering grin and began to arrogantly slither away. I was still so scarred I didn't even have the strength to swing the boat paddle at him. I whimpered and whined "Kill him, kill him," but Charlie was laughing so hard at me by this time, he was having difficulty keeping his britches dry.

My fear turned to wrath as the snake went looking for some smaller fisherman to swallow whole. I managed to throw my tackle box at his retreating form and in so doing, lost some of the best bass plugs and crappie lures ever made. If I ever came closer to getting snake bit, I don't know it. And I don't want to know it.

That was a close call!

I nearly got hit head-on by a black kamikaze reject, driving a loaded pulp wood truck in Mississippi. The only reason a 500 pound Bolivian Jaguar didn't jump the 30 feet into our boat and eat me and Wallace both alive was because he just didn't want to. I still do not know why my '65 Mustang quit spinning and sliding on the ice just before going off into oblivion on Lolo summit.

I have had a few close calls of the type that leave you wondering why you are still alive. But the closest one I ever had came after a steak dinner at the Sizzler in Spokane. As we lingered over a cup of coffee and pie, the chairman of the executive committee to whom I answer informed me "We'd like you to plan to move to Florida as soon as possible."

Now, I'm not really sure God made Florida. If He did, it was on His day off when He really didn't feel too creative. I have a personal belief that everything south of Tallahassee was just what He had left over after He finished the rest of the world. Florida, in its natural state, is nothing but an oversized sand box. And you know what cats do to sand boxes. Scrub pines, palmetto bushes, rattlesnakes, alligators, mosquitoes and hurricanes are about the only contribution this place can offer to interrupt the monotony of too much sunshine, too much heat and too much humidity.

Add 44 million tourist a year (mostly damnyankees) to the natural discomfort of the place, plus another who-knows-how-many folks fleeing Castro's paradise and you end up with overcrowded freeways, plastic playgrounds, McDonalds and K Marts where no English is spoken and a murder rate that's the highest in the U. S. A. Florida!

Some of the dearest and closest friends I have on this earth live in Florida. I don't know why but they do. And I live as close to them as I want to unless they decide to move about 3,000 miles west by northwest. I even enjoy visiting them occasionally but the best thing that ever came out of Florida is United Airlines flight 721 to Denver. A quick change there and you can be in Boise for lunch and back home in time for supper with the Pole Creek Ridge Rod, Rifle and Reuben Sandwich Society.

But the idea of moving to Florida struck pure terror in my heart. If a grown man crying for 3 months sounds silly to you, I bet it's because you believe the lies those Madison Avenue ad men have told you about Florida without ever having been there yourself. But just going to Florida is only half the problem if that much. It's the idea of having to leave Eastern Oregon.

I always said I'd live here until God got mad with me and when He did, you could tell how mad by how close to Florida He put me. Well, when the committee finally told me they had changed their mind and wanted me to stay put, it was the closest thing I could imagine to a Russian roulette revolver clicking on an empty cylinder. "A new lease on life" comes nowhere near explaining the feeling!

There's nothing that will make you appreciate getting up on a bitter cold morning long before daylight to join the Pole Creek Ridge Gang on their annual Christmas tree cutting trip like realizing the alternative. You could be going to a Florida supermarket to pay an exorbitant fee for a shedding dead tree that was cut from an Oregon hillside and shipped out a month earlier.

Yes sir, that was a close call! But I tell you every time I step outside in the crisp cold of a new morning, look out our front window at the most beautiful mountains on earth, smell the freshness of a fir thicket, look eyeball to eyeball at a big mule deer buck, eat one of Peg Leg's Reuben sandwiches by a camp fire, throw a tamarack log on a crackling fireplace, stretch out in the afternoon sun on a ridge overlooking the Sumpter valley, listen to an old bull elk's bugle echo across Mt. Ireland or a Canada goose honking from an otherwise empty sky, I appreciate it more than I ever thought possible.

A close call? A new lease on life? A stay of execution? It was more like a reprieve from a sentence of exile!

And there was no way of expressing my thanks to God at this Thanksgiving season for the privilege He has given me of remaining here in my beloved west.

PART II

EVERYONE IN FLORIDA IS FROM SOMEWHERE ELSE

EVERYONE IN FLORIDA
IS FROM SOMEWHERE ELSE

"If you don't quit talking so bad about Florida, God is going to send you there to live," Harriet warned me.

I've got to admit, it was a threat worth taking heed to. I should have taken it much more seriously. My wonderful wife is one of the most rare breeds in America. She is a native born Floridian. And unless you are in or near the maternity ward of a hospital in the Sunshine State, all you have to do is ask and you'll see what I mean. The first question one usually asks upon meeting someone in our state is "Where are you from?" In answer to that query you'll get answers from Albania to Alabama, from Boston to the Bahamas and from Utah to the Ukraine.

Harriet was born in what is locally known as U C L A -the Upper Corner of Lower Alabama. She was born in Mariana, Florida but she didn't like it and moved out of state when she was just over 6 months old. And she has always harbored the hope of returning to her native land one day.

I was almost 11 years old the first time I came to Florida. My Daddy finally saved enough money to take the family for a vacation on the beach near Panama City. All the hype had me expecting a few days in land as magnificent as heaven itself. Boy! Was I surprised? No one told me that the sun was so hot that it could literally burn you sick. I mean water blisters, fever and all. The sulfur water from the faucet smelled so bad you couldn't even stand to brush your teeth with it, much less drink it. And the water in the Gulf of Mexico was too salty for anything but swimming- if you could stand the sea weed and the jelly fish that stung worse that a bumble bee. I may have been just a barefooted country boy but I decided then and there that anywhere more than 10 miles south of the Georgia line was too close to Cuba. And if I never went back to a Florida beach the rest of my life, it would suit me fine. I have never changed my initial assessment.

And now, as a permanent resident of the Geriatric State, I have found even more reasons to warn you to avoid this piece of real estate. Someone once asked me about dangerous places I've been. "What is the most dangerous mission field you have ever been on?" a lady asked me in a church in Michigan. I didn't hesitate a minute to tell her that I *now live* on the most dangerous mission field in the world. And I began to check off my list of reasons for saying so:

- At least four kinds of poisonous snakes;
- Several breeds of so-called non-poisonous serpents with some that grow to a length of 18 feet;
- A wide variety of poisonous and non-poisonous spiders, some as big as your hand;
- Lions; Bears; Wild hogs;
- Alligators; Crocodiles;
- Killer whales; Sharks;
- Disease carrying mosquitoes, ticks, fleas, fire ants and parasites;
- Hurricanes, tornadoes and more lightening strikes than anywhere on earth, except Viet Nam, I'm told;

And those are just the natural disasters. To that list you can add:

- More people die of cancer than any other region of the world;
- More children are killed on bicycles;
- The highest crime rate on our continent;

But the most dangerous hazard we endure is the big luxury vehicles that invade us in an annual winter migration. Our roads are filled with elongated Lincolns, big Buicks and slow-cruising Cadillacs. Add to that an infinite number and an untold variety of oversized motor homes and recreational vehicles. They have an insatiable desire to drive in the left lane. They will blow you off Interstate 75 when they are headed south thru Georgia. But when they get to the Florida state line they immediately shift over to the left lane and slow to a crawl. They maintain this pace until they once again hit that state line going north in April. When you approach one of these northern visitors on a narrow state road, you would swear there is no one driving. Until you see a little blue Q-Tip peeping up thru the steering wheel, trying to see over the hood.

When the snow birds from New York, Michigan, Ontario and Ohio do not overload our roads we are inundated with rental cars and mini vans loaded with large and loud families all going to see our greatest attraction: the rats that have grown to be six feet tall: Mickey and Minnie!

Why, even this dynamic Disney duo are transplants from California. I guess their kind of life-style isn't so unusual where they come from.

Like I said, everyone in Florida is from somewhere else. Even the Native Americans, the so-called native Floridians, our Seminole Indians were chased down here from Georgia by their Cherokee cousins!

WAKING UP
IN THE WRONG WORLD

It is a tragic day when a fellow has to rush through the state of Eastern Oregon. Fortunately, I am in no hurry.

You need not look on a map for our state but it is there and just as real as any of the 50. It may not be a political entity but Eastern Oregon is a state of mind. It is that grand and glorious portion of the Creator's handiwork where the skies are bluer, the clouds more colorful, the creeks run clearer, the grass is greener and the air is fresher.

The boundaries lie somewhere east of a line from Mt Hood to Three Finger Jack and west of the Snake River. It is bordered on the south by a desert and on the north the Colombia River marks it's extent.

The black ribbon, which takes you from Pineville through Mitchell and the John Day valley, is divided into only two lanes by a broken yellow line. The interstate crowd uses such unfortunate terminology to describe it "narrow, crooked, rough" before which they usually add the qualifying "too".

The city slickers use even worse language in describing this beautiful country. They call it "desolate, empty, barren". Yet such is the taste of the unappreciative.

But wait a minute something is wrong.

I was in my usual place, the drivers seat of my pickup. It had me headed north to bring my Mother down to visit us for a couple of weeks. But somehow I had the strange feeling that I was the victim of someone's dirty joke. Was I in a space transporter? I was in the wrong place headed in the wrong direction. And not just because I was going to get someone's mother-in-law.

I should be driving with the windows down to catch the cool evening breeze blowing down from the Blue Mountains. Instead, the windows are shut tight and the air conditioner is running at full bore.

And even at that, it is barely able to keep me out of the heat stroke zone. There should be the pungent sweet smell of sagebrush in the air. Instead there is the dank odor of mildew and mold with which the rainy season leaves its signature in places even beyond the reach of its tropical downpour.

I should have heard the howl of the coyotes last night. Instead, my night was interrupted by the disgusting yells and yowls of the cats chasing cockroaches that were bigger than their kittens. Judging by the size of some of those creatures we have seen around our place, I would not be surprised if it was the cockroaches chasing the cats!

But this is September. In fact, it is the weekend before the Pendleton Roundup. A fellow should be polishing his boots and getting his rodeo tickets ready for the country's greatest edition of America's best sport. Instead, the signs along the highway are advertising the Steinhatchee Seafood Festival. I don't have a thing against seafood but it is a poor substitute for a Cowboy Breakfast at the fair grounds. There should have been at least a hint of frost along with this mornings sunrise instead of the heavy and sticky morning mugginess of a leftover summer that has long outworn its welcome with me.

The signs along my route of travel should be announcing sweet sounding names with precious memories like Halfway and Haines, Pendleton and Prairie City, Sisters and Sumpter, Burns or Bend or best of all my beloved Baker City.

But this ribbon of asphalt takes me through wide spots with names so strange sounding that you have to study to pronounce, if they are meant to be pronounced. There are tongue twisters such as Sopchoppy and Estiffanulga. It is no wonder that the natives around here even call Wewahitchka simply "Wewa". I guess there are at least a dozen folks who have a return address that tells the world that they live in Bloxham. Then there are road signs that make you wonder if they are serious when they point to Two Egg and Redhead.

Yes sir, I was in the wrong part of this country. But finally one sign gave me hope. There it was, big as life and announcing Umatilla. Now, I am not especially fond of that Oregon town. And after one particular football game a few years back, I didn't really care if I never went thru there again. In fact, it would not have bothered me if they had given it to Washington. At least their hometown referees. But when you are as homesick for Eastern Oregon as I am, even Umatilla sounds good.

Wouldn't you know it? This is Umatilla, Florida! The little Lake County town where a 77-year-old man was attacked by an alligator in his own pond. I guess these Umatilla towns have more in common than just their name, after all.

The farther I travel on the crowded highways, the more lonesome I am for the wide-open spaces where a fellow can see the sun when it sets. How I would love to sit and watch an old flop-eared mule deer doe with twin fawns. I want to hear a hawk scream across a timbered ridge and watch an elk grazing thru a lodgepole patch. I want to feel a rainbow trout on a lightweight fly rod. I want to smell buck brush and fresh-cut timber and smoke rising from a campfire. I want to taste a fresh cup of strong coffee brewed on a ridge overlooking a ghost town that used to be Whitney.

Please don't think me totally discontent. My sweetheart and I love the new house God has given us in central Florida. We are extremely happy to be involved in the ministry our Lord in His wonderful grace, has extended to us. But I do miss the fascinating beauty of the Oregon outback. I miss the familiar faces at the Sumpter Nugget and One Eyed Charlies. I miss the seldom-traveled trail from Marble Creek Pass to Twin Lakes.

I was not a native born Oregonian. But the gorgeous grandeur of the Baker Valley, the Elkhorns and Eagle Caps was born in me and is, to this day, borne in my heart. And anyone who enjoys its people, loves to hike its forests, drives its roads and drink from its streams is bound to understand the gnawing agony of homesickness that occasionally grips a fellow whose body may be in Florida but whose heart is in the Pacific Northwest.

You see, it finally happened. The hammer hit on the loaded cylinder. I was transferred to Florida. I had asked God for a letter as written confirmation should He ever exile me from the best country in the country. And who would ever expect a written letter from God?!

But there it was! A fax message no less. Well, it was not signed by God Almighty but it may as well have been. It actually came from the executive committee to which I answer. It said that since I was the only member of the leadership committee I served on left in North America; and since they needed a representative in Florida, would I please bring my family and move to the swamps?

Of course, I laughed when I showed it to Harriet. Look what a mistake they have made. I won't loose any sleep over this because there will be another fax in my box tomorrow morning saying that I should ignore their previous cruel joke. They would admit that they had made a terrible mistake.

And I did. I went to bed and to a sound sleep. Until about 4 A M when the Lord woke me with the realization that we had some serious business to attend. I went to my study and began reading my Bible.

Now, I didn't hear any voice nor see any visions or anything of that sort. But I did get a very definite message from somewhere. I had traveled all over the English-speaking world, into churches, youth meetings, missionary conventions, colleges and seminaries recruiting foreign missionaries. For nearly 20 years I had been challenging Christian men, women, youth and even children to obey the Lords command and GO into all the world. I had encouraged them to leave houses and lands, families and friends and go to the uttermost parts of the earth. And some of them to whom I spoke actually did and are now in some pretty remote and isolated jungle locations in Africa, South America, Southeast Asia and a couple of Islands of the South Pacific!

And I wasn't even willing to go to Florida!?

So before I could renege on my commitment to do whatever our Lord asked me to do and go wherever He wanted me to go, I went to the fax machine and sent a message that I had read somewhere. The original was to the War Department in the earliest days of World War II from a wounded veteran of the first World wide conflict. My message went to the Executive Committee to which I am accountable. That message simply said:

Available. Dependable. Expendable. Say where. Say when.

We packed our worldly possessions into a U Haul truck, loaded our little Subaru on a tow-behind dolly and moved to Florida. Lots of folks have told me that God really didn't want them on the mission field; He just wanted to know that they were willing. That always sounded to me like a lame excuse for not answering the call. But at this point I was desperate enough to try anything. As soon as we got out onto the Interstate, I pulled off on the shoulder of that big super slab and had another conversation with the Lord. I told Him that this should sufficiently show Him that I was *willing*. And if He was just playing games with me, could I take the next exit and return to this beautiful little city and plan to live out the rest of my days in the land that I love?

I didn't get an answer there so we headed east and south. I tried that prayer again before we crossed the Snake River into Idaho. And again at the Wyoming state line. And every one of the 9 state lines we crossed in our move to Florida. The fact that I now reside in the geriatric state should tell you that God wasn't joking. And if you want to know where we lived before moving here, you can follow the heel marks where I drug mine for 3,085 miles.

Yes, we now live in Florida! And we have found it to be home. Our Lord has given us a great church family, good neighbors and friends as dear as anywhere in the world. And of course, 5 of our 6 GRAND-children live here. And all but one of them is native born Floridian just like their grandmother!

SNAKES DON'T DIE 'TIL SUNSET

The quietness of her voice belied the panic that I now know was in her heart. At the time I did not even know my own name. Even the sun knows that this was far too early an hour for anyone to be up and about. But there was enough light beginning to show in the sky to turn it into the color of dirty wash-water after a load of Wrangler jeans. "I hate to wake you this early in the morning but there is a snake in our shower," she said. "Will you come kill it?"

As soon as she said, "snake", I was as close to fully awake as you can get in less than the flick of a rattler's tongue. But just as soon, I knew this must be her idea of a joke. She has pulled a lot of dirty tricks to get me up early before but this beats them all. She was more than a month and a half too late for April Fool's day. She must have had a nightmare. Too much barbecue sauce on the ribs last night. But not a real live, honest to goodness snake. Not with her still standing there by the bed, within 6 feet of the bathroom door. In the same house with an alleged serpent.

Now if you knew my wife, you would know that she has an intense hatred and fear of snakes. The mere mention of the S-word in her presence puts the speaker in danger of her exceeding great displeasure. She nearly flunked biology in high school when she found a picture of a king snake in her textbook. If her friend Camile had not taped the 2 pages preceding it to the 2 following pages, she would have been happy to drop out of school her sophomore year. She was able to pass freshman history in college only because she talked the professor into allowing her to change the required term paper subject from Christopher Columbus to the Battle of the Bulge. "Columbus" was too close to the lengthy article on "cobra" in the encyclopedia.

I can honestly report that years, maturity, nor any amount of appeal to human reasoning have diminished her firm conviction that any kind of serpent is a personal embodiment of the devil himself. She even threatened to cancel our cable subscription when she saw that Australian bloke handling one of the cursed crawlers on the Discovery Channel.

For her to calmly report that "There is a snake in our shower" meant only one thing. There was a strange woman in our bedroom. I don't know who she is nor can I imagine how she got in here. I probably should warn her that if she used that S-word again my wife would wake up and wash her mouth out with soap. But I was the only one left in the bed and that strange woman looked exactly like my wife. And she sounded like her even if she did not talk like her. Harriet would never simply report the presence of anything even resembling a snake. News of that magnitude is always presented with wide eyes, rapid and shallow breathing (if any breath at all), high-pitched voice of increased volume and blood pressure so elevated that it is obvious to the observer. More than once I have been conscripted in that manner to kill a deadly 6-foot section of rope. Yes, when it comes to snakes, Harriet is irrational.

And that may explain why she always calls for me to kill one. If she were able to think at a time like that she would know that I am the wrong one to call. You see, I am the only one in the known world who is more afraid of snakes than she is.

She, of course does not believe that. She is persuaded beyond change that she holds the title of "most afraid". She claims to have irrefutable proof. I will look at a picture of one, she points out. And I have even been known to get close enough to one to kill it.

Like I said, Harriet is irrational. Her dislike of serpents is based on what she vows is a natural and sane, even if blinding, deafening and numbing fear. My fear is more reasoned, rational, theological and Biblical. God damned the serpent in Genesis when he allowed himself to become the physical body of Satan and lead our parents Adam and Eve into sin. And the curse was that he would be forced to crawl on his belly. The fact that to this day, snakes have not evolved legs is ample proof to me that they are still under the curse of God. As such, I take it as my Christian duty to hate snakes.

As I said, my fear is not only Scriptural but also reasoned and rational.

No other creature in nature has such strange and mystical powers. Everybody knows that you cannot kill a snake as early in the day as Harriet wanted me to dispatch that monster in our shower. Well, you can "kill" him but a snake won't actually die until sundown. Any country boy can tell you that many times we have killed a snake and put him on a fence to wait for the sun to set. And yet before dark that snake we knew we killed dead would revive and crawl off when we were not looking! And we knew he crawled off because we couldn't find him. Just because there was no track, even in soft sand around the fence posts, was not evidence that a hawk had found his supper.

And what other creature do you know can actually change his size so miraculously and so quickly? I am eyewitness to the fact that a snake nine feet long and as big around as my leg when he is alive can shrink himself to the size of my finger and make himself no longer than my forearm within minutes after being killed. And the very next day (when Harriet tells it) that same snake will have grown to his original nine feet, added three or four feet in length and be as big around as my waist. Obviously, it is by demonic powers which they all posses.

Since I knew that there was no real snake in the shower, I walked right in there, face to face, eye ball to toenail, with that belly-crawling, dirt-eating devil. Then I was wide-awake. I quickly slammed the door to the shower stall while screaming for Harriet to "get me something to kill this thing with."

I shouldn't have called. Harriet was already out the front door and headed for the car when I caught her. "Go check the girls' rooms. See if he swallowed one of them. Tell them to lock their door and don't come out unless I tell them to."

My 16-gage Ithaca pump is always loaded with birdshot and stands ready in the closet. If I had been rational I would never have grabbed so light a load in so small a gun. If I had time to think I know I would have loaded the 12-gage Browning with slugs or double-0 buckshot. Bravely, I went back into the bathroom and closed the door behind me. If he got me, at least he would be locked in here and my family would be safe until the sheriff got there.

As I took careful aim thru the glass door and was just ready to squeeze the trigger, it dawned on me that the shattering glass might deflect the shot and my enemy would attack me before I could pump another shell into the chamber. You know of course that snakes are faster than lightning and can jump up to six or eight times their actual length. Or so Harriet tells me. Actually, I think it is farther than that.

So I rehearsed in my mind how I could throw open the door and shoot at the same time. How I wished the shower door were not glass so he could not see me coming and prepare his defense. Even if I missed a direct hit there would be enough pellets ricocheting around the tile walls of that bathroom that one was bound to get him. It never occurred to me what all of that ricocheting lead could do to me. But it did dawn on me that the reverberating roar of a shotgun in a closed bathroom would probably burst my eardrums.

Carefully backing out the door, I kept the gun aimed at the shower in case he opened the door from inside. At six feet long, he could easily reach up to the handle if he chose to. I was putting my earplugs in when Harriet peered thru the front door. "Here, kill him with this shovel".

I told you she was irrational. A vision of hand-to-hand combat with an eight-foot snake in the close confines of a shower stall is not my idea of a way to start a new day. Probably because of some unconscious and stupid notion about a man protecting his family, I agreed to give it a try. But only if Harriet would back me up with the shotgun. She promised to guard the door and shoot the first thing that came out without first giving the password.

Again locking myself back inside the bathroom, I tried to formulate a plan of attack in my mind. I stood on the toilet and reached for the door. If I could coax the monster out of the shower stall, I would have more room to swing the shovel at him. With his ten feet of length and my 240-pound frame we would fill that whole bathroom in our winner-lives, looser-dies battle.

Maybe I can reach him over the shower door and attack him from above. It was a good plan. I just miss-calculated the distance you can lean with a foothold no sturdier than a toilet lid. The lid went one way, my feet another and the rest of me in a completely different direction. My shovel bounced off the tile inside the shower stall and

I hit the floor. My glasses fell in the toilet and I dived in after them even before I could get my breath.

"Are you alright?" Harriet screamed. With the wind knocked out of me, all I could manage in reply was a grunt.

"Kill him, Honey. I know you can do it". There was more pleading than persuasion in her voice.

Looking thru the glass shower-door, I could not determine which was the shovel and which was the snake. And I was not about to reach for either one until I could get my glasses back on. Even then the distortion thru the glass made it difficult to determine one from the other. I sat there on top of the counter and tried to reason. The one standing in the corner with the head down was most likely the shovel. The crooked one on the floor was probably the snake.

As I retrieved my weapon back over the door, I saw my chance and struck my first blow. Miraculously, it was enough to send the morning intruder back to the pits of hell from which he had slithered into our morning. Following the fatal blow, he shrunk to a fraction of his actual size. I put his eleven-inch body into my shovel and reached for the door handle.

"Don't shoot, Harriet. I got him."

"What's the password?"

"I can't remember. But trust me. The snake is dead."

"I don't believe you. You lied to Eve and you'll lie to me. Where is my husband?"

"Harriet, please. Let me out of this bathroom" I begged.

"You come out of that door and I'll shoot you."

"Mom, I think it is really Dad. Maybe you should open the door and see," our daughter pleaded.

Well to make a long story short, Harriet only let me out after Sunshine went outside and looked in thru the bathroom window. I hung the snake on the fence and the last time I looked he is still there.

Of course, it isn't dark yet.

BRAHMA BETSY
GOES SHOPPING

"There is no such thing as a dumb question." I found myself repeating to one of my own inquiring Bible college students the statement that one of my professors had said to me in the past millennium. Sounded good to me when he said it so I just passed it on. And in a classroom I guess I'll stick by our statement. It is dumb to have a question about the subject you are studying and *not* ask it.

There is no such thing as a dumb question.

For the most part, I guess I still think that is a true. But then

Have you ever listened to a television reporter interviewing a cowboy? Or TV reporters in general, I'm afraid. It really comes out when you get a hot-shot young lady trying to startle the world with her brilliance and unseat Barbara Walters with one exclusive interview. Or maybe even worse, some young man still wearing diapers beneath his GAP wardrobe that wants Charlie Gibson's job next to Diane Sawyer every morning.

Just put that young'un in front of the camera with a microphone that looks like a big glob of black ice cream and send him out to the scene of breaking news. But don't listen to the frivolous questions he comes up with if you are interested in real *news*. Comic relief, maybe. But not sanity.

"Were you afraid when that African gorilla grabbed you from between the bars of his cage?"

"Did it hurt when you shot yourself thru the foot with that nail gun and fastened yourself to the side of the garage?"

"Do you believe this serial killer was really trying to harm his victims?"

You can't help but wonder if Reporters School has sent these people out with a book of dumb questions. If they ever went to Reporters

School in the first place.

Here is what I mean.

It was one of those hot, humid days in what the rest of the country calls spring. But here in Florida it was warm enough to qualify as a full-fledged Fourth of July heat wave in Atlanta. At least that's what it felt like it was going to be when Charlie and the boys unloaded the horses from the trailers at the Volousia County pasture where they have a couple of hundred head of mostly-Brahma cross-breed cows and some of the meanest bulls of any breed in captivity. As Darrell called the dogs together and started out south with Charlie, Brady and Earl circled off toward the east and entered the woods. Hopefully the herd wasn't too scattered and they could get them bunched and thru the gap, across the field and into the pens early. There was a good crop of young calves to be sorted, branded, vaccinated, castrated and a few old cows who had lost ear tags that needed replacing as well as a worm treatment for each animal.

It was not long before a cow and calf here were pushed over to the half-dozen or so there and the whole bunch was moving in the direction they needed to be. Not unusually, one old mama Brahma decided to show her offspring the fine art of aggravating the cowboy and headed of at a diagonal from the bunch. That's when the cowboy has to show Baby Brahma why Florida cowboys carry a bullwhip. And if she is particularly stubborn or fast enough to get into the thicket ahead of the horse and rider, she learns the tenacity and seriousness with which the well-trained cow dog follows cowboys instructions to encourage her to return.

When the rebellious pair hit the fence line, baby turned north while mama went thru the second and third strands of barbed wire and lit out in the same direction but on the opposite side of the fence. And when the dogs got serious about turning them, Miss Baby turned and high-tailed it back toward the safety of the herd and left mama out in the cold cruel world beyond the fence.

"Leave her alone, she won't go far with her calf in here. We'll get her later Charlie," hollered.

"Git back here, Roper! Come here Purple!" Darrell yelled at the dogs. Now you don't separate cow dogs from the game they love best by just a suggestion, but after several commands and a well-placed sting of the whip, the dogs dutifully returned to the bunch and the cowboys pushed them on towards the pens.

After lunch at the closest bar-b-que joint, the crew loaded back into the pickups and Charlie called to Brady on the radio, "Ya'll go around the back way and see if that ole cow is still out or if she came back thru."

When they met at the pens and got ready to resume work on the herd Brady reported "She musta made it back, we didn't see her anywhere." He untied his horse and swung up into the well-worn championship saddle hed won in a rodeo long past. And no one had time to give it any more thought as the scorching sun beat down on the dusty and loud and busy pens and chutes where 200 head of aggravated cows were being separated from their calves.

The operation was progressing according to schedule until the blue and white cruiser from the Daytona Beach Police department pulled up to the gate. "We got one of your cows up here. Guess it's one of yours. She's up at the Publix parking lot and they finally got her tranquilized. Could you come see if she's yours and remove her if she is?"

What are you going to tell the local law? Sorry, were busy. Just bring her over here and we'll take care of her. Yeah, an eleven hundred pound sleeping Brahma cow in the trunk of a police cruiser? I don't think so.

"What happened, officer? Why'd you have to tranquilize her?"

John Law was grinning so big it was hard for him to hold back. And by the time he told about the damnyankee from New York and his first encounter with a Florida swamp Brahma, the officer was almost doubled over with laughter.

Seems mama departed the fence line and found her way into a nearby village of suburbanites, complete with long Lincolns of New York registry, SUVs with child restraint devices and big Buicks from Boston and Detroit and a sprinkling of native born citizens. As she explored new territory from yard to yard, someone called the law. By the time the first cruiser arrived she had made her way to the end of the street and was cornered by a wooden fence surrounded by well-trampled hothouse transplants and slightly abused bushes and trees.

The fancy new pickup truck had Florida plates betraying the fact that he really was from up "Nu Yark". But as soon as he opened his mouth there was no doubt about his nativity. And with the self-confidence that seems to have been bred into those of his native state, he offered to take the situation in hand. "I was raised on a farm. Ill get her for you," he assured them. And with a cocky swagger to match his braggadocio boasting he headed toward her. "Piece of cake", he guaranteed the onlookers.

Mama jerked her head around to size up her approaching assailant. It was just curiosity at first but as he sauntered onward, she wheeled around and squared up on him like a linebacker ready for the kill. Her head went down, snot bubbles exploded from her flared nostrils as she gave a warning snort. She pawed the manicured turf just two or three licks before beginning her charge.

Mr. Smarty Pants, in a sudden flash of good sense rare to his species, determined that discretion was by far the better part of valor. As fast as youve ever seen a Yankee move, he showed her nothing but elbows, shoe soles and hip pockets. One step and he was on a dead run for his new pickup. Unfortunately for him, mama had already gotten her full speed and was gaining rapidly.

If the truck had been just a few yards further, he would have been dead meat. But luckily for him he reached it only one step before she reached him. In a leap that would have won any Olympic jumping event he left the ground and sailed toward safety.

He almost made it. With perfect as if calculated timing, she lowered her head and heaved upward, catching him in mid-air. With just the right amount of pressure applied under his feet, he was propelled thru a full cap-over-shoe soles somersault. Completely clearing the bed of the pickup, the yank landed on hands and knees and rolled like a bowling ball. Fortunately, the truck was between him and her shielding him from an immediate follow-up attack that she was anxious to press.

But just because she couldn't see where he was and he couldn't see her did not remove from his panicked mind the need for full and immediate retreat. When he stopped rolling, he began crawling on all fours, thru the rose garden with mulch flying as he scratched and scrambled, clawing for traction. Clothes ripped, hands, face and ears scratched and bleeding from the thorns, "our I-was-raised-on-a-farm" imported expert managed to scramble under the nearest front porch. Finally safe from a real but no longer present danger.

Brahma Mama had already headed to town!

I don't know what happened to the would-be stock handling yankee. By this point the officer telling the story was doubled up in laughter and unable to get sufficient breath to complete the story.

"We'll" take Brady's trailer to bring her back in," Charlie said and he and Darrell headed for town. Their wandering cow was not that difficult to find. In his typical dead-pan expression Darrell said "I hope nobody else in Volusia County needs a cop!"

Charlie whistled. "I didn't know Daytona Beach had that many cops", he said as they turned into the parking lot at the Publix supermarket. "What's the fire truck for? And why the ambulances?"

Deputy sheriffs, city police and even a Florida Highway Patrol or two had gathered. Then they noticed the various television news vans with antennae towering above the planted palms; radio station news crews and newspaper reporters.

"This is going to be interesting!" Charlie sometimes shows signs of being a real prophet.

And sure enough, when they parked and began to approach the circle of flashing blue lights, all they could see was a wad of blue and black uniforms punctuated by an occasional yellow firemans slicker and the white jacket of the ambulance attendants. And in the middle of the crowd lay a soundly sleeping Brahma crossbreed cow!

It is still unclear as to what route she took from the neighborhood but it was more than evident that she had taken complete charge of the entire strip mall when she got there. "We'll back the trailer up to her," Charlie said. "Did she hurt anybody or break anything?"

"Nope, said a deputy sheriff." Unless you count scaring the snot out of several shoppers, "he added with a chuckle. "You should have seen folks scatter when she walked up to the door at super market." I guess it looked too much like the squeeze chute when the automatic door opened cause when it flew open she balked and wheeled around back down the sidewalk. But not before there were abandoned grocery sacks, and shopping carts all over the place. "Why, when I drove up there were folks scattering like quail in every direction. There were folks on the roof of their cars and one fellow on top of that coke machine", he pointed. "I even found an empty wheel chair! Lord only knows where that fellow went!"

By this time Brady and Earl had arrived. They lassoed the cows front and hind legs and threaded their ropes thru the stock trailer and out the front. Charlie mounted his palomino Fancy and Darrell booted the stirrup of his gelding. "Awh shucks" said the deputy. "You don't need them horses. We'll just pull her in."

I told you there were a lot of cops gathered. Enough to pull that sleeping cow, all eleven hundred pounds of her dead weight up into the trailer!

When the horses were finally loaded behind Sleeping Beauty and the tail gate latched, one of those aforementioned TV reporters with his GQ clothing, salon coiffure cut and city slicker intelligence confronted Charlie.

"Sir, can you tell us why this cow would do something like this? "

Now remember, we are talking about no such thing as a dumb question. So Charlie gave an intelligent answer to this less than brilliant query. "Well, son, you know women. Ole Betsy just wanted to go shopping!"

But wait, our reporter isn't finished asking his (not dumb?) questions. He turned to Darrell and asked a question with much same lack of sanity. "What do you think she was going to do?"

And in the same seriousness as the reporters inquiry, Darrell answered "I just don't know what that crazy female was planning. We told her to go to McDonalds and instead she headed for Wal-Mart!"

There may not be any dumb questions. But if there are, you can be sure that a news reporter will ask them!

FLORIDA COWBOYS

When I say Florida, what came to your mind?
Did you picture a cowboy, the real working kind?
I bet you thought Disney and maybe Shamu,
Universal Studio and the Space Coast, too.

Florida Cowboy, you think that's a joke,
"Cause cattle should be worked by a Texas cowpoke;
In Oregon, maybe or Idaho,
Montana, Wyoming or New Mexico.

Cowboys and Indians, where the buffalo roam?
That's away out west that they call home.
Cattle need prairies and wide-open spaces,
Not beaches and swamps and tourist places.

From Canaveral to the moon, you easily believe
But cowboys in Florida are hard to conceive;
Astronauts and the space shuttle crews,
Get all the press and make lots of news.

Florida is famous for the Coppertone Tan,
But who'd expect the Marlboro man
On a Florida beach in his cowboy boots,
Among all those beauties in Bikini suits?

Seafood, you know we'll produce for you,
Yet, what about the beef that's in your stew?
You may not have known it until just now
But it probably came from a Florida cow.

Not far inland from that coral reef
Is a corral that's filled with Florida beef,
And hard working cowboys who are willing and able
To furnish a great roast for your dinner table.

At Daytona racetrack they show off their Harley
But 3 miles south there's cowboys like Charley,
With Brady and Darrell and the rest of the crew,
Maybe Christie and Carrie and the cowgirls, too.

They're working hard in the tropical sun,
Making sure there's a patty on your hamburger bun.
Cause gators and orange groves ain't all we boast.
We've got cattle from coast to coast.

That sirloin so good you cried when you ate it?
A Florida cowboy probably gets credit.
That steak would be grazing in a cypress swamp still
If it hadn't been shipped to your backyard grill.

There are cowboys in Florida! I tell you no lie,
And way up there in the sweet by and by,
I wouldn't be surprised on the Lord's dinner plate
There'll be a juicy T-bone from the Sunshine State.

PART III

LEST WE FORGET
THOSE MEMORABLE MICE!

LOOSIN' AIN'T EVERYTHING, BUT IT SURE BEATS NOTHING TO REMEMBER

We all call Aunt Anne "Sister", the traditional Southern name for the oldest girl in the family. She is more than a decade beyond that octogenarian birthday when women begin to be proud of their age instead of trying to hide it. I guess none of us men will ever understand why women spend the first seventy years of their lives scared to death that someone will find our how many birthdays they have actually had. They begin, some as early as their early to mid twenties denying, disguising and even lying about their birth date. But, at the four-score mark something happens to them and they are just as scared that you won't know how old they are. It is likely that within the first paragraph of meeting a new person, or even an old friend they haven't seen in a while, they will proudly make sure that you know their actual age.

My own Mother rather emphatically scolded me the other day, "You need to start treating me with a little more care. Remember, I'm an 80 year old woman!" I told her that when she started acting her age, I'd treat her like it. An old lady with that many birthdays should be riding a rocking chair instead of driving her own Buick. I never know whether to call her up in Georgia, back at home or down on the beach in Florida. You'd expect a grandma her age to be sitting and knitting instead of walking 3 miles every morning with the mall walkers, or flying off to Germany to visit her grandson!

Well, younger women just don't like to tell their age. And I guess the writers of the Scriptures understood that. There are only two women in the Bible whose ages are told. And they did not tell it, God did. But even He didn't disclose it until they had both passed their eightieth year.

But getting back to Sister. Someone asked her why she talked so much about things in the past. She wisely, and with a twinkle in her eye answered that, at her age, "most of my life is in the past! At 99 years old, I sure don't have a whole lot of future to talk about!" But the twinkle in her eye and the love of life so evident in her aspect belies the fact that she's really planning a lot more birthday celebrations!

I guess it was hearing her say that which made me begin to realize that life is pretty well made up of memories. A lot of our rumination is time spent just remembering -times, people and events in our past. Quite a large percentage of our conversation is talking of things we have done, places we have been, people we have known, sights we have seen or stories we have heard.

Memories. It is what life is made of.

And it is not just the good things we remember. Some of us have a past we would desperately like to forget. Some have incidents and episodes we wish had never happened. All of us have a nasty little memory of something we hope no one else will ever know about and we wish we could forget ourselves.

Like that football game in Ontario. The one Goose and Tom would like to have removed from the record book, or at least erased from this ole Dad's memory. Which ain't gonna happen! It was one of those things that got so absolutely bad/awful that you had to view as if it was a script created by the writers of the Three Stooges cartoon.

It was the first game of the season and both our boys, Tom and Goose had made the starting lineup. Goose was the offensive center and defensive line backer. Tom was defensive back and on the special teams unit. I had watched lots of their pre-season practices and for some reason, my reports gave their Mother reason to believe that the NFL would have scouts there for the game. Even though it was only the junior year for our high school boys, we were more than optimistic.

We won the coin toss and took it as an omen of great things to come. The coach had instructed his captain to elect to receive the ball on opening kickoff. With the electrifying excitement that parents seek, usually unsuccessfully to control, my wife and I stood for the occasion. There was no way we could sit down.

When the Ontario kicker couldn't even get the ball to the deep backs, we knew this game was ours. But this would probably be the last time he'd get to kickoff, seeing as how we'd be the ones scoring all the points and doing all the kicking from here on out. It would just be a matter of time before their coach would have to pull his wimps off the field and forfeit the game. (As it turned out this idea of forfeiture would come up again -but not just exactly as we imagined.)

The ball barely got to the mid-backs and right into Toms eager grasp. Unfortunately, their rushing linemen could outrun a kicked ball and managed to get to Tom just a heartbeat later. Tom fumbled the ball! Heck, you would too if you saw a couple of Bradley Fighting Vehicles with the speed of a NASCAR racer bearing down on you! How those fellows got passed our supposed blockers no one has yet been able to determine. But there they were. And just because Tom no longer held possession of the football was no immunity. The first two hit him at full speed and the other one recovered the ball on our 35-yard line.

They scored on the next play.

Regrettably for us, on the ensuing kickoff their kicker had not improved his abilities nor lengthened his output. But this time their rushing linemen had slowed a step or two and Tom had plenty of time to fumble the ball and even pointed to it in hopes of slowing their pace or diverting their attention. It didn't work. They still hit him with enough force and energy to kill an NFL pro. And the only reason their teammate who recovered the ball didn't sprint the 35 yards to paydirt was that three of his own men hit him from behind by reason of sheer momentum.

But they managed to score on their next play.

To the relief of everyone on our side of the field, the coach sent in a freshman to replace Tom on the next kickoff. No one, I might add, was more excited at the inevitable decision than our poor boy who had had enough of a beating in two plays to last him the whole game, if not the whole season. The freshman gladly entered the game with the confidence and cockiness that only a freshman who has never survived attempted murder could exhibit. The coach had strictly warned him that if by some miraculous intervention from above he managed to get possession of the ball, he was to immediately fall on it and guard it with his life. His wise decision to obey his coach was probably the only thing that saved his young life. He did receive the kickoff, he did make a good catch and he immediately fell to the ground in the fetal position and he did maintain control of the football.

This collection of Ontario heavy equipment that had previously mangled Tom simply piled on the terrified freshman. (I think he wisely quit football after that game.)

And now we finally had the chance to show our stuff. Our offensive team took the field and, trailing by only 14 points, they were eager to avenge the setback and kick some tails!

Goose delivered the football to the eagerly waiting hands of our quarterback Andy Ballard who dropped back to pass. A solid wall of offensive linemen suddenly appeared in his face as if they had been teleported thru our supposed defensive line. He managed to step back another couple of paces before they smothered him. Seven yard loss on the play.

This time Andy wasn't quite as eager to take the ball from Goose but he was more than eager to hand it off to his running back. Unfortunately, he was unable to do so before one of their blitzing linebackers hit both of them, wrapped them up in a bear hug and slammed them to the turf. Two other linebackers and an undetermined number of rushing linemen joined him. When the referees were finally able to get the mess untangled, the ball was marked down for an additional 5 yard loss.

Rumor has it that our boys earned a 5-yard delay of game penalty because Andy couldn't call a play in the huddle. Every back and each of the receivers adamantly refused to let him call any play that would result in the ball coming into their hands. And Goose swears that he had a difficult time in getting Andy to take the ball from him when he tried to center it. The supposed pass play resulted in Andy being buried 9 yards behind the line of scrimmage.

Mercifully it was 4th and 21 and we finally had an opportunity for Chance Warren to punt us out of trouble. He stood on the 10-yard line and waited for the snap. Gooses handling of the ball would have been an outstanding performance if it had been a forward pass. Later,

Goose gave Warren a hard time for not even trying to catch the ball. "Goose, you centered that thing so high over my head, I couldn't have hit it with a 12 gage shotgun!" he declared.

Heck, he threw the ball farther backward and between his legs than Andys longest completed pass of the season! The ball sailed over Warrens head and into the end zone. And there wasn't even one of our men willing to contend with the onrushing linemen for it. They fell on the ball there and the following extra point fixed the score at 21-0 and there was less than 2 minutes off the clock!

I don't think I need to give you much more information about the remainder of the massacre. Let it be sufficient to say that it just got worse.

There was even a committee of mothers that met the coach on the way to the locker room at half time and begged him to take our boys to the bus and get out of town while there was a still hope of them surviving the game. My wife led the delegation! They argued that forfeiture was much to be preferred to a mass funeral.

I don't remember much about the games of the remainder of the season. I do recall that we maintained a perfect season. We almost slipped up and ruined it in the last game when we nearly scored on Hermiston.

But I will never live long enough to forget that opening game!

Yes, sir. Winning ain't everything. Even loosing a lousy game in Ontario beats having no memories at all.

THANKS FOR
THE MEMORABLE MICE!

There are some disturbing hints that I may have passed that invisible line between middle age and seasoned senior. When the young lady gave me the senior's discount without asking to see my drivers license I had to admit that maybe I have crossed the line. A kid who is older than my own teenager told me "you remind me of my grandfather." I am old enough to be concerned that young folks today waste too much money and time on the video machines at the mall and young enough to want to be right in there with them.

Middle aged? You try to define that term. At least give me a ballpark guesstimate as to the chronological period in years that we are talking about. It has to be a relative term. My Dad was an old man all my life. And my Mother is an 89-year-old teenager who just traded in her Buick for a classier and sportier Chevy and took off to Georgia. Alone.

Perhaps the best definition of middle age is old enough to know better and too young to care.

Contemplating an article in the mornings Daily Commercial newspaper makes me wonder if I just might have grudgingly arrived in that land of middle age. The report is that some students released white rats at the performance of the spring play being presented to the student body during school hours. It was the premier before being opened to the public in evening performances.

In response to this report I find myself torn in a dilemma. Part of me says that 10 days suspension and not being allowed to participate in graduation exercises is just and deserved punishment. But the other part of me says that these kids should be rewarded. And I can give you several reasons why.

There are too many muggings and murders, riots, rapes and robberies to report. This newspaper and all the others could use some comic relief.

And believe it or not, that prank actually encouraged my confidence in the younger generation. Finally we have evidence that there are teenagers with creative minds. Just when I was tempted to believe that the extent of their imagination was wrapped in toilet paper on some teacher's lawn, some of them break out of the mold. We were rolling lawns when I was a kid, just after the Constitution was ratified. Before indoor plumbing.

And what about the economics of these enterprising youth? In the best American tradition of thrift and wise management of money, these boys purchased rats that were on sale rather than pay the full price. Maybe we should appoint them to the school board. Or Congress.

Did you notice that all the rats were captured? Ready to recycle. The principal admitted that he doesn't know what to do with them. Ask the boys. I bet they could offer him some ingenious and maybe even some profitable suggestions. Don't be surprised if they recommend selling them to Eustis High seniors. Probably make a profit on the deal and help alleviate some of the pressure on the school board's budget.

The old man in me admits that it could have been dangerous. After all, a teacher even got bitten by one of the rats. But you know as well as I do that the public schools of every city in America, with their halls patrolled by an armed cop would be happy to settle for nothing more threatening to worry about than the risk of a rat bite.

We older folks need to point out to the younger generation that four fun-loving young fellows should not disrupt a production that many had worked hard to perfect. But the show did go on two more times.

Is it the kid in me or is it the old codger I am becoming? Or is it my seasoned seniority that tells me that these boys may have done us all a big favor? They gave us something to remember about the Umatilla High School class of '92. After all, life is made up of memories.

And it does not have to be a winning game, a perfect performance or a great production. It could be the rats at the spring play. These enterprising young men with a creative sense of humor have given us some memories. I can guarantee you that we will remember the rats for generations after we have forgotten the name of the play they enlivened!

I think that creativity and ingenuity like that should not only be encouraged, it should be rewarded.

Thanks, fellows! Because life really is made of memories.

DID JESUS SUBSCRIBE TO *PROGRESSIVE FARMER?*

The Scriptures are clear that Jesus of Nazareth was a carpenter. Not only was he raised in the home of Joseph, a carpenter but He was Himself identified as "the carpenter" (Mark 6:3). Yet I cannot help but believe that His heart was really the heart of a sodbuster with manure on His sandals! I suppose today we would call Him a "wanna'be" farmer.

And maybe He inherited this from His heavenly Father. Why, for example, would the Almighty Creator, Who could have built a perfect city without traffic congestion, without overcrowding, that was crime free, pollution free and politician free, start off by creating a *garden*?

Why did the Heavenly Father not arrange for the birth of His Son in the finest of places and select a stable instead? Born among farm animals instead of theologians! Why was His birth announced to sheepherders instead of priest or pastors?

In His earthly teaching ministry, there is neither one parable nor story from the carpenter's shop. But Jesus frequently used stories from agriculture and animal husbandry to illustrate His messages. He spoke of seed and sowing, He talked about planting and cultivating, about pruning, about reaping and the various size of crop returns at harvesting time. He talked about farm owners and hired workers. He spoke of wise farmers and foolish farmers, of fertilizers and fruit trees.

And I can't help but believe that if the *Farm & Ranch Living* or *Progressive Farmer* magazines had been published in Israel about 2000 years ago, Jesus would have had a subscription to guarantee issues in His mailbox every month! And He would probably have given His mother a subscription to *Country Woman* as a Christmas gift.

The professionals down at the seminary with their subscriptions to theological quarterlies and scholarly journals of religion and religious magazines may not know how to take this. But I was raised by a service station owner who, among other similarities to Jesus, was a "wanna'be" farmer. We did not live on a farm but we did live in the country. We cultivated no crops, but we always had a garden. We raised no livestock (except for one attempt at a goat which nearly cost Mother's sanctification and my status as favorite -and only son). We always had fresh eggs from our own hens. And I learned to drive on a Farmall Cub tractor.

But every month there was a new and interesting issue of the *Progressive Farmer* delivered to our house. Many an hour I've seen my Daddy reading articles about nematodes or hybrid seed, hog prices and beef breeding. To tell you the truth, the only thing I remember him reading besides his Bible and the newspaper was his *Progressive Farmer*. I just wish he had lived long enough to have seen the creation of *Farm and Ranch Living*.

I suppose I'm just a chip off that old block. And the delivery of every issue is almost like a visit with my Daddy. He's probably sitting on the porch up in heaven these days, chatting with some Old Testament wheat farmer or some New Testament shepherd. And when he notices me reading "Tractor Talk" and "Uncle Len" or vicariously visiting some fascinating ranch near Plush, Oregon, he just grins and remembers that the fruit doesn't fall far from the tree!

And I have the firm suspicion that if our Lord were born in our land today, His nativity would occur on a cattle ranch in Eastern Oregon or on a sheep farm in Western Montana! Or maybe, just maybe He would have chosen a cotton plantation in South Georgia or even a cattle operation in Central Florida!

Oh Little Town of Wagontire? kinda has a nice ring to it, don't you think?

BEAR MEAT, BUTTERBEANS AND THE BOARD OF EDUCATION

You would need to have taste buds native born in the deep south with perhaps a bit of red Georgia clay still between your toes to really appreciate a saucer on the stove with left over bear meat and a cold biscuit. But the vivid memory of that feast fit for a prince still makes my mouth water. And I was a teenager before I knew it really was not bear meat after all. It was salt-pork. The kind we called 'streak-o-lean' or 'fat-back'.

It was so salty that Mother had to cut it in slices like bacon and soak in water over night. Then she'd drain and dry it before she covered it in flour and fried it in grease. She called it 'bear meat'. I have since eaten quite a bit of bear from a black bear- and as delicious as my wife can make that taste, it is not even in the league with Mother's delicacy.

At exactly 3:35 this afternoon the memory of that special stove with it's manna from Mother crept in from my subconscious and I was suddenly 3,000 miles and 50 years away. I was 8 years old and just getting home from Miss McWorter's second grade at Edgewood School. Bounding in the back door, I never stopped until I had checked what was in that oven.

And regardless of what she had cooked for dinner, and she always cooked dinner, she had set back at least a biscuit or two, maybe no more than a cup of butterbeans or black-eyed peas, perhaps some brown gravy and a pork chop or a piece of cornbread. But there was always something leftover from dinner that she had put aside just for me.

Now, I never did like school. Schoolwork, that is. I was usually bored to death with the material that those wonderful ladies were hired to teach rascals like me. Schoolteachers were always ladies in those days, by the way. And they were the finest caliber of people God ever let live. The ones I had for the first six years thru Miss Julia Ann Pomeroy, were right up there with the preacher in purity and goodness. And they usually surpassed Einstein in brains, too.

So I don't mean that I was as smart as they were. But I had usually read all the books in the room within the first month of the new school year. So when she got around to teaching the rest of the class, I had heard it and decided for myself what was worth remembering and what wasn't. Looking back at my report cards, which I have forbidden my children to do under penalty of death, you will notice that between what those ladies thought worth remembering and what I thought was important, there is a great gulf fixed.

So, being bored with the class material, I had to invent something to entertain myself which I never had any problem doing. There was a problem but it was Miss Penland's or Miss McNeil's or whoever happened to have been sentenced to guard me that year. And being just and gracious ladies they in turn shared whatever difficulty they had with me by inflicting a fair and equal punishment. Far surpassing Old Testament justice of an eye for an eye, they always gave more than they received.

I vividly recall one rainy day in the third grade when I received three spankings (we called them whuppins) for the same offense. Miss Nix had told us not to get on the swings during recess because of the puddle of water that had collected under every one of them. There was no way to swing without getting your feet soaked.

Although I was not the smartest kid in the class by a long shot, I did have a certain amount of reasoning power even at that young age. And knowing by experience that I was far too agile to have to worry about getting *my* feet in the water, I calculated that the swing was worth the risk of getting caught. Having learned so much in just two previous years of scholastic experience, I'm still amazed that I hadn't learned that there was always at least one warden on duty during recess. And ole' eagle eye nailed me by the third time my Buster Browns hit the puddle.

She promptly delivered me to Miss Nix who not only canceled my leave and sent me to the room, she tanned my hide with that stick she kept just for fellows like me. When the rest of the class came in, I was sitting by the pot-bellied stove drying my socks. My problem began to get serious when the principal, Mr. Turner, stuck his nose in the door and inquired why I was sitting by the stove barefooted. When he heard the story he invited me to accompany him -barefooted- to his office where he applied his own board of education to the seat of my knowledge.

This time I no longer sat by the stove. But I did stand there until my socks were dry. My shoes never did get dry before school was out. So Miss Nix sent a note home to explain to my Mother what had happened and to assure her that I had been sufficiently punished for the crime.

But that didn't save me from Mother's addition to my suffering. My parents had a standing rule that if we got a spanking at school, we got another one at home. They had this archaic notion that the teacher was always right and deserved to be supported. So when Mother finished reinforcing Miss Nix and Mr. Turner, I slept on my stomach that night. My only consolation being that Daddy didn't add the weight of his support to their decision with a spanking of his own.

To this day it doesn't seem to bother my parents one bit that my basic civil rights were violated that pre-Civil Liberties Union day. The Constitution of the United States of America plainly states that a person cannot be punished twice for the same crime. The wise writers of our Constitution never even considered the possibility that a citizen of this great and free nation would be subjected to *three*, count them - *3*, punishments for the same offence.

Unfortunately, I chose to swing in the rain before I read the Constitution.

THE WAY THANKSGIVING SHOULD BE

I had the high and holy privilege of speaking to the entire student body in chapel at one of the largest Bible Colleges in Canada. The only problem was that it was on Wednesday, the day before Thanksgiving. And as great as that honor was, the prairies of Saskatchewan were not the place to be on this last Thursday in November. We always had a noon meal with all the students in our training center in Baker City and I didn't want to miss it. A missionary traveling with me wanted to get to his family down on the Snake River in Idaho so we departed the Moose Jaw area as soon as I finished preaching. Crossing the Canadian/US border just before dark we headed diagonally across that huge state of Montana. It was already after sunrise when we entered Idaho as we alternated driving throughout the night. I left Duane in a snowstorm in Twin Falls and drove on home alone. Arriving home exactly 24 hours after beginning this mad rush to get home in time for Thanksgiving dinner, I was exhausted.

My first big problem was trying to stand up after 24 hours in a little Subaru! When I finally made it to the living room couch I had about an hour for a nap before the meal was served. I fell so soundly asleep that Harriet couldn't wake me up to eat!

I missed that one. But to tell you the truth, as good as they are, no Thanksgiving has ever made it up to the standard of the ones we knew in Chattahoochee. I guess it is because they just do not make Thanksgiving the way they used to.

Thanksgiving is the warmest season of the year. Oh, I do not mean weather warm. Not even back-up-to-the-stove warm. But heart hugging warm. Thanksgiving is family reunion time.

Thanksgiving day should begin in the pre-dawn with Bo, Buddy and Bill (three of the greatest fellows in the world you could call cousin), sitting under a tree with a gun across your knees, frost on the leaves, waiting for the sun to wake the gray squirrels. It is the heart-stopping explosion of a covey of quail erupting under your feet as you cross a barbed wire fence with a sack of bushy-tails. If you have never been squirrel hunting on a frosty morning, you don't have as much to be thankful for as I do.

Thanksgiving is a mid-morning visit to the sugar-cane mill powered by an old black mule that walks a million miles and never gets anywhere. But the endless path that he plods encircles a press that extracts pure liquid sugar. This juice from Blue Ribbon cane was nectar that attracted boys the way the syrup attracted yellow jackets. The juice was cooked over a wood fire in a pan that was 4 feet by 20 feet by 6 or 8 inches. This long, slow process required tending day and night in order to maintain the proper temperature and produced the most delicious syrup that ever drowned a biscuit. If you never got your cane syrup directly from the mill, you don't have as much to be thankful for as I do.

Thanksgiving is the discomfort and inconvenience of having to dress up in your nice clothes when it's not even Sunday, just to go eat dinner. But the meal that the women have been planning and preparing for days and the kinfolks who will come from four states will make this trip worth the trouble.

Thanksgiving is not Thanksgiving unless you are at Uncle Stanley's place. Uncle Stanley was over 6 foot 4 but when you are five years old looking up, he was ten feet tall. In every way, he was as close to a Biblical patriarch as will ever live in a 20th century white shirt and tie. His wife was just plain Frances to everyone except her grandchildren and an undetermined number of nieces and nephews who called her "Sank". By the time a boy was 10 he could expect to be taller than she was, even in her high heels. Yet folks looked up to that wonderful woman as if she were as tall as her husband.

Thanksgiving should be a gathering of uncles and aunts who came in an endless variety of sizes, shapes and types. They were newspaper editors, schoolteachers, atomic energy scientist, farmers and insurance salesmen, football coaches, mailmen and storekeepers and even a farmer or two.

If the generation of aunts and uncles was multiple in numbers, the cousins were infinite. Coming in every size from brand spanking new babies to those who were bringing their new husband or wife to the first family gathering. Thanksgiving should be having enough elementary-age cousins for a world class game of hide and seek in the old barn. There should be enough early-teen cousins to get the very latest and most accurate information on any movie or rock star known to man. Enough high school and college cousins, male and female, for a fun game of tag football - as much of a game as you could have in Sunday-go-to-meeting clothes.

Thanksgiving is the yet unsolved mystery of new faces that appeared every year. They were always introduced, as this is your cousin so-and-so from somewhere. "Why, back when we were your age… " and then they proceeded with some grand and glorious story which brought warmth to their voice and a sparkle to their eye.

If you don't have so many kinfolks that you don't even know who everybody is at the family reunion, you don't have as much to be thankful for as I do. But thanksgiving shouldn't really be a word all by itself.

Thanksgiving-dinner was the real occasion of this November Thursday. Solomon in all his glory never faired so sumptuously. Arthur and his round-table knights never ate as scrumptiously as that feast which was simply called Thanksgiving Dinner. Without question, the most warm and wonderful place to be this side of heaven itself was Sank's kitchen the hours before the main event. Every square inch of counter top, table top and both inside and top of the stove was loaded with bowls, pans, pots and platters of taste-tempting delights that tormented the taste buds with the realization that you had to wait just a little longer until cousin so-and-so got here or until the giblet gravy was ready. But the coffee urn was ready and there was an endless parade of kinfolks coming thru while Sank puttered around the stove and filled you in on the family news. When that feast was spread there was a variety that still dazzles the memory. Perhaps the least appetizing entree was the turkey. But there were also chickens, ham, roast beef, pork and sometimes-wild game. Once Uncle Tol even brought a big pan of the most delicious barbecue that brought many coming back for seconds. But it nearly cost him his life when some of the aunts later found out that it was actually Goat.

Folks outside the Deep South would never be able to comprehend the manifold variety of vegetables. There were peas: black-eyed, pinkeyes, purple hull, ladyfinger, Crowder and butter peas. Snap beans, butter-beans, baked beans and lima beans. The sweet potatoes were baked, souffled and candied. Turnip greens, collard greens, squash fixed a dozen ways, boiled okra and fried okra, creamed corn and corn on the cob.

There were potato salads, chicken salads, tuna salads and enough tossed salads to feed Gideon's army. Made-from-scratch biscuits, hot rolls and cornbread. The butter was not margarine and the variety of jellies, jams and preserves was infinite. Big pans of cornbread dressings were made plain, with apples or with oysters from Apalachicola Bay.

The only thing allowed on that lavish table store-bought and just out of the can was the cranberry sauce. And even then there were always three or four different kinds. If you were still ambulatory after the main course, the deserts would remedy that. Pumpkin pies and apple pies; cherry, blueberry, blackberry, strawberry and huckleberry pies; lemon icebox pies and peanut pies; chocolate, banana cream, coconut and the Cadillac of all pies: pecan. Peach, apple, cherry and pear cobblers and banana pudding. A six-layer Japanese fruitcake, old fashioned fruit cakes, German chocolate, cherry-pecan and coconut cakes. Aunt Ruth's four-layer chocolate cake remains to this day as the state-of-the-art.

If you haven't eaten Thanksgiving dinner at Uncle Stanley's, you don't have as much to be thankful for as I do.

But you could not eat a bite until he had called all the family together for the blessing. His youngest daughter Jane was as talented as she was beautiful. In a voice as rich as Gabriel's trumpet she sang "Bless This House" with such sweetness and feeling that caused many sniffling noses and tears wiped from almost every eye.

Then he prayed. And when Uncle Stanley prayed he didn't read a message to the Deity. He didn't just say a prayer or repeat a blessing. When he prayed, he talked to His Lord. If you didn't have an Uncle Stanley pray for you, you do not have as much to be thankful for as I do.

Times change and Thanksgivings change. The old black mule was replaced by a power takeoff on a John Deere tractor; the family grew so big the gathering had to be moved to the county park; Jane's piano accompaniment became a cassette player; Uncle Stanley went on to heaven and Sank is in a nursing home.

But some things will never change. The ever loving, heart hugging warm memories of Thanksgivings the way they used to make them. I hope that you have as much to be thankful for as I do.

———————————

first published in the *Democrat Herald*, Baker City, OR

THE NEXT BEST THING
TO BEING THERE?

The telephone company says the use of their long distance services is the "next best thing to being there". That ain't true and somebody ought to tell them so. I just talked to my Mother in Georgia with one of their desk model instruments so maybe I'll be the one to burst their Madison Avenue publicity bubble.

The Mother I love so dearly is 3,000 miles away sitting in that cozy corner of her kitchen with my sister who is more of a dear friend than just a sister. I can almost see them in my vivid imagination. Almost taste the coffee from one of those pale blue cups she has had since pre-memory days and still uses (the ones I probably tasted my first brew from). I can smell the lingering fragrance of oven-made toast. Picture the warm spring sunshine coming in thru the sliding glass doors from the tiny patio of her apartment. See the hanging basket and planters of blooming flowers that are the ever-present evidence of that special lady's handiwork wherever she has lived.

What I see in my mind's eye is far too vivid to be just imagination. It is memory. Precious Memories. What I wouldn't give to sit in those white chairs at that kitchen table and eat a pile of boiled peanuts that she had put back in the freezer just for the day her son came for a far too infrequent visit. To watch her putter around that kitchen as she gets the turnip greens, black-eyed peas and squash casserole cooking for dinner.

Thank God, she never fed her family "lunch". You can take lunch in a paper bag to eat on the tailgate of a pickup as easily as you can eat it at a clean kitchen table with real cloth napkins. What my Mother prepared for our noon meal was never thrown-together-between-commercials, cold sliced substitute for real *dinner*. And when I talked with her just now, I declare I could almost smell the pork chops frying. My mouth waters at the mental smell of that pan-fried cornbread. And my heart longs to be able to join, in person, those loved ones.

Next best thing to being there?

In a pigs eye! Compared to the warmth of love and fellowship and security of a real Mother's kitchen, there ain't no second best! Anything else is just a cold piece of plastic held to your head. It is just an electronic reproduction of sound in your ear. It is a gut level hollow spot that can only be satisfied with a piece of warm buttered and toasted pound cake and a kiss on the forehead by a beautiful old lady who says with a satisfied smile, "It's so good to have you children home!"

Next best thing to being there?

There is no "next best" to the fulfillment of that third (or is it the fourth?) cup of black coffee while you get caught up on news of Johnnie Mae, Mrs. Massey, the Bundricks and Uncle Kieth's children. The pure excitement of Aunt Ruth coming in the front door with a big hug and a fresh chocolate cake. Beautiful Beverly dropping by with two young men that any one would be proud to call nephews. But Robert and Beverly have had a new baby since last time I was home. And there is no substitute for seeing and holding my newest kin in person.

I must not have been any more than the 4th or 5th grade but I can vividly remember a P. T. A. meeting I had to attend at Edgewood school because Mother was president. My Daddy read a poem that burned into my memory that night and I have since read many, many times:

"It takes a heap o' livin' in a house t' make it home,

A heap o' sun an' shadder, an' ye sometimes have t' roam

Afore ye really 'preciate the things ye left behind,

An' hunger fer 'em somehow...."

And even though it isn't the house we grew up in, the one built by Daddy and decorated with memories that will last a lifetime, that bright and cheery little apartment is home now because it is where my dear Mother and Daddy live. And wherever they are is really home. And there is no next best thing to being there in person!

YOU CAN NEVER GO HOME

I came home to Georgia this week. But somehow I didn't really come "home." Such changes have taken place, it makes me realize how disconcerting it would be if you did not know the Lord.

Everyone must have, to maintain any security feelings or assurance, some permanent and changeless things. I sit to write this on a spot that was the corner of a pecan grove with a cement water tank when I was growing up. Today it is a coin-operated laundry on the corner of a shopping center. The old swimming hole on bull Creek now has the support pillars for the freeway in the middle of it.

There used to be good hunting in the woods off Morris Road. Shoot a gun there now and you're liable to kill someone's kid on a tricycle. The fields I plowed with a tractor now grow brick and mortar houses.

And, our old house? Another family lives there now. But you'd hardly recognize it the way they have added the patio, changed the driveway and cut some trees. No, you can't go "home."

I was in Miss Pomeroy's sixth grade before I met a real live, honest-to-goodness Yankee in person. And here in the laundry is a couple with Illinois plates on their car and a young soldier from Pennsylvania. And Miss Pomeroy's sixth-grade classroom was blown away in the tornado a few years back.

I went by to see the sweetheart of our senior class. Jenny Lind is still beautiful, but as grandmother she no longer wears a ponytail and bobby sox. Another one of the skinny kids we went to high school with is now the distinguished city attorney.

But Mother and Daddy are still here. Well, they have an apartment in town. But my 185-pound, hard-working daddy is now a 90-pound invalid who has to be tended like a baby. And my once healthy, happy mother is now a discouraged and insecure senior citizen who must hire someone to help her care for Daddy.

You can't go "home."

But Wynnton Baptist Church is still there! The place where I was baptized and ordained to the gospel ministry. The Shepherd building is named for my uncle George Will and one stained glass window is dedicated to the memory of my Godly grandmother Gordy. They are still there.

Still there, for now anyway. The building is for sale and the congregation already has raised some of the hundred of thousands of dollars they'll need to buy the new property out north of town to build the new building. So you can't even go to the "home" church.

But really, the home church is not bricks and chandeliers, stained glass and pews anyway. The home church is Mr. Melvin Hargett faithfully leading a Sunday School where boys and girls and their parents could learn the word of God; Mrs. F. E. Massey leading the Intermediate department year after year in Vacation Bible School; Hines Preston and M. C. Bundrick teaching God's Bible to boys (liberally illustrated with bird hunting and bass fishing stories); Rufus Matthews, Bussey Gordy, the TEL class and Harry Gray – yes, that is the real Church.

And yes, they are still there. Maybe not physically. Actually most of them are in heaven today. But they are just as real and just as effective and just as influential in my memory and in my ministry. Because, what they really built was not just brick and steel, steeple and stone. They also built into the life of one young boy a hunger for the Word of God, a love for his people, a desire to serve the King of kings and a security in Christ that far surpasses anything this world can offer. And for these things I shall eternally be grateful to our great and changeless God. "For here have we no continuing city, but we seek one to come." (Hebrews 13:14.)

ISBN 141203080-3